MURDER AT 113 LOMBARD STREET

TONY RUANO

eRIGINAL
Books

Published by Eriginal Books LLC
Miami, Florida
www.eriginalbooks.com
www.eriginalbooks.net

Copyright © 2010, Tony Ruano
Copyright © 2015, Cover and Design: ENZOft Ernesto Valdes
Copyright © 2015, Of this edition, Eriginal Books LLC

First Edition: November 2015

Registration number: TXU 1-686-512
Effective date of registration: April 15, 2010

ISBN-10: 1613700830
ISBN-13: 978-1-61370-083-9

Translator: Ally Campbell
Editor: Olga Arroyo

Murder at 113 Lombard Street

Tony Ruano

For Adria Lourdes, always my lady.
For Adelkys and Anel.
For Lucas Rafael Antonio López Bello, Tonín,
who found the murderer.

CONTENTS

PROLOGUE

Through the fog he made out the police officer, patrolling the roundabout. He shouted as loudly as he could. The officer followed the direction the cry came from and approached the person; he stopped his bike and asked:

"Is there something wrong, sir?"

"Quickly!" said Paul. "There's no time to waste! Look for a vehicle to carry two seriously ill patients to the hospital! But don't waste any time, please. I'll wait for you at 113 Lombard Street."

The policeman arrived with the ambulance twenty minutes later. When he saw that no one was waiting for him, he thought that he'd been the victim of a practical joke or someone had wanted to divert or distract him from his job. Only curiosity, when finding the door to the house open, brought him in and up the stairs. When he reached the living room, he was shocked. He could not believe his eyes. There, writhing on the floor apparently having severe seizures was the man who warned him earlier and five others, including a girl. He picked up the girl in his arms and hurried downstairs. He placed the fragile little body on the stretcher and ordered the driver:

"Take her to the hospital and send three more ambulances immediately! There are five more people in the same condition up there. This looks very serious. Hurry!"

**

The patient load had been so severe at the hospital that night that the doctors on duty failed to make the connection between the six people who recently arrived at the hospital suffering with the same unmistakable symptoms of choleric gastroenteritis. But the senior admissions doctor found it suspicious that all of them lived at the same address, but only two of them were in very serious condition; for this reason, he called the hospital director to discuss his suspicion that they might be dealing with a collective poisoning. Given his colleague's hypothesis, Dr. William Rust decided to visit the patients. He carefully studied the diagnosis and urgently ordered more laboratory tests to determine the causes of the phenomenon. Forty minutes later the lab report arrived at Dr. Rust's office.

CHAPTER I

Mrs. Mary Gautal's guest house was hosting the celebration of the return of Luisa Hayen and her little daughter Annie, after an eight-day stay in France visiting her aunt.

Luisa was still amazed as she remembered her old aunt and her stay on French soil together with her daughter; but it happened and what mattered most was that she was able to hold her close once again and, despite her years, the aunt seemed to be in very good health. In addition, the French air had served as a tonic to her fragile nerves. The dreadful nightmare of the death of Annie's father when the girl was not yet three years old; the financial ruin, caused by the loss of all business inherited from her husband, a product of the ineptitude of his then manager and now her life partner. Alfred Hayen, had left her exhausted, destroyed, unable to make a decision and in full dependence on her current husband.

To celebrate, Mrs. Gautal had prepared a special dinner: baked bread rolls with butter, vegetable soup, steamed potatoes and vegetables, roasted turkey in apple sauce and for dessert, vanilla cake. As an accompaniment, they would serve the wine that Luisa had brought from her trip.

Dinner was served when the Donalts showed up in the dining room.

"Sit at the table, please! Let's not let the food gets cold," said Mrs. Gautal.

"We will not allow it," Luisa replied holding the freshly uncorked bottle of wine in her hands. "This feast can't possibly be allowed to cool down. It looks too good."

"Thank you, Louise. I'm glad that you like it. This meal is in honor of your return."

"I appreciate it but I don't think I deserve such an honor," said Luisa.

"You fully deserve it and a lot more, darling," exclaimed Alfred Hayen just as he was entering the dining room holding little Annie by the hand.

"Wow! I'm glad to see that your relationship has gotten better." Jeannie Donalt pointed out, turning to Alfred Hayen while taking a seat.

"As far as I'm concerned, my relationship with Annie has always been great, Mrs. Donalt. It's just that she hangs on to issues that lack any importance, those merely childish fancies that'll fade away as she matures."

"Let's sit please! Let's sit down to eat!" said Mrs. Gautal while she placed a steaming tureen on the table.

The bread rolls disappeared quickly from the basket. Everyone enjoyed their soup slurping it greedily and then moved on to savoring the turkey with roast potatoes and vegetables, Paul Donalt remarked:

"Aren't you going to taste the French wine, Luisa? It's gorgeous!"

"I still haven't overcome my aversion to alcohol, Mr. Donalt. Thank you."

"It's a shame. You're missing something quite exquisite," said Jeannie Donald and demonstrated by taking long sip from her glass.

"Do you want to try some, Annie?" asked Alfred the little girl.

"No, thank you. Mom says that alcohol is not for girls."

"And that's true, honey. Alcohol is not good for your health," stressed Luisa.

"Just a sip won't do any harm Luisa, please," pleaded Alfred.

"No, and that's final!" Luisa's sharp response was heard around the table.

"What's the cake made of?" asked Annie. "It's Chocolate?"

"I'm afraid it is vanilla flavored cake this time, but I know you'll enjoy it anyway," answered Mrs. Gautal.

"Of course I'll enjoy it," said Annie. "Do you know that I don't really like chocolate that much?"

Everyone laughed at Annie's kind remark. Paul Donalt went to the kitchen and returned with the chocolate cake. He sliced it and offered a generous piece to Annie. After dinner, Mrs. Gautal invited her tenants to move to the living room while she stayed behind to tidy up the dinner service. They all accepted except for Luisa who offered to help with the clean up. Shortly after, the two women joined the rest in a lively conversation.

"That was a delicious dinner!" Alfred remarked while fixing his gaze on the burning flame of the matchstick he just used to light his cigarette.

"I'd say it was an exceptional feast!" added Paul playing with Annie's curls.

"By the way, Luisa, tell us all about fashion in France," asked Jeannie Donalt.

"Did you visit any of the fashion houses?" asked Mrs. Gautal with an almost childlike curiosity etched on her face.

"No, unfortunately I didn't have time. I focused my visit on my aunt Annie. She was feeling poorly and disheartened and wasn't in the mood for fashion," answered Luisa.

The conversation stopped. All eyes met in a sign of understanding. Luisa lowered her head and kept her eyes fixed on the floor. Silence dominated the room for a moment and it was Paul Donalt who decided to continue the conversation by asking:

"Luisa, where exactly does your aunt Annie reside?"

"My aunt lives in the region of Provence, Paul. It was a long trip there and I was exhausted when I arrived at her house."

"Well, I don't tire that easily and, when we arrived, I went for a walk with auntie Annie and her yellow cat and everyone greeted me and blew me kisses, offered me candy and promised me all sorts of things. Everyone asked me where I lived and wanted to know everything about me and all of my friends and ..."

"Enough, beautiful, you're going to dazzle everyone with this outburst. Take a deep breath and then speak slowly. Do you think you can manage that?" Luisa intervened talking to the girl.

"Yes! OK, but I didn't yet have a chance to tell them of the freshly baked cookies or the chocolate cake my aunt made just for me, nor of the delicious cheeses that she offered me daily, nor of the bitch who had eight adorable puppies all of the same color, or that horse ..."

"Well, Annie," interrupted Alfred. "Would it be okay with you if we give your mom a chance to tell us how it went there for her and give us her impressions of your trip?"

The girl didn't hide her disgust at Alfred's interruption. She looked down, frowned and tucked herself even more under Paul's arm, which made her feel sheltered. Luisa stared for a long moment and, after a brief silence, began to speak:

"Aunt Annie is doing very well despite her advanced age. As for my impressions, I can say the trip was invigorating and inspiring. The French people seem to have overcome many of the problems created by the war and there is talk of rebuilding the country; new dreams arise ... and so ... At least that's what I could feel during my few conversations and what I drew from reading the newspapers. You know, most days Annie went for a walk

17

through the nearby villages and sometimes spent hours and hours out before coming back into the house; I took advantage of her absences to read and catch up with the local news. I had plenty of time read and I read a lot, because Annie didn't stop taking her walks for a moment."

"I see! So that's what you've been up to, little girl: you went for lovely walks while we were here, all bored to death, huh?" asked Paul Donalt in cheerful tones, trying to lift the little girl up from the simulated boredom in which she found herself.

"Yes. I had a lot of fun, but I brought you the pipe you asked for," said Annie as she ran down the corridor leading to the Hayens' private rooms.

"What's the story with the pipe, Paul?" asked Luisa. "Annie didn't give me a break for a minute during the trip talking about this pipe. She even insisted that she would not return without it. What did you promise in return?"

"Oh! Nothing important," said Paul. "I told Annie that if she brought me a French pipe, I was going to give her a red-haired doll."

"Ah! I see! But I think your pipe will cost you quite a bit. Don't you think, Paul?" inquired Luisa.

"Don't worry, Luisa, I was planning to give her the doll anyway," replied Paul.

The girl's hurried footsteps on the hallway came through to the hall. With her face glowing, Annie gave the small pipe to Paul who, touched, was listening to the girl exclaiming breathlessly:

"Look! Look! Here it is! And look how cute the

drawing is! It's sweet! Really nice, Paul! Do you like it? Tell me Paul! Isn't it truly adorable? Tell me! Don't you just love it?"

Paul inspected the pipe excitedly. Then, directing a smile to the girl, he picked her up and sitting her on his lap, kissed her cheek.

"Thank you, Annie. I like it very, very much!"

"Are you joking Paul? Do you really like it?" exclaimed Annie applauding.

"How can I not like it when it's you who bought it for me, beauty?" replied Paul.

Jeannie Donalt stood up from her chair and, without excusing herself, ran down the hall sobbing. In her room she collapsed on her bed, reproaching herself for not having been able to give her husband a child.

CHAPTER II

It was five o'clock in the morning when the alarm clock rang. Alfred awoke. Luisa and Annie were still asleep. He dressed hurriedly and went to the bathroom then returned to his room and left the wet towel on the back of the chair making sure that mother and daughter were still asleep before tiptoeing into the kitchen where Mrs. Gautal was waiting for him.

"Good morning," said Mrs. Gautal when she saw him. "No kiss for me?" she asked reproachfully noticing Alfred Hayen's apparent coldness.

"Looking for trouble? Don't you ever think that they could hear us? You must remember that Luisa is back now," said Alfred as he went to sit at the table.

"Forgive me. I didn't know you were so afraid of her."

"No, it's nothing like that. But you must understand that Luisa has the upper hand. If she finds out about us, she'll ask for a divorce."

"That would be most convenient for everyone, don't you think?" said Mrs. Gautal.

"Don't be so silly! Don't you know that if she orders a review of how her estate has been managed, I'll go to jail for the rest of my life?"

"If you keep thinking like this, we'll never be able to lead a normal life. You need to decide once and for all what you want to do with the rest of your life!" replied Mrs. Gautal.

"Calm down now! You're being impatient. Give me a little more time and I'll find a way out of this mess!" said Alfred.

"And how long will I have to wait, huh? Until we're too old for anything?" asked the exasperated landlady adding: "I assure you I'll find a solution to this situation. You can count on it!"

"I imagine you're capable of anything!" said Alfred as he took the last sip of his coffee.

At that very moment, Luisa Hayen returned to her bedroom, having listened to the whole conversation that took place between her husband and her landlady.

The clock struck seven when the Donalts came into the dining room.

"Is breakfast ready? Believe me I have a huge appetite," said Paul while seating himself comfortably at the table.

Jeannie glared at him. Paul unfolded the napkin, placed it on his knees, sat in the chair and sliced a piece of bread. He looked up and saw that his wife was still nailing him with a hard stare, so he threw out a question trying to relax the tension floating in the room:

"Are we having breakfast alone today?"

No answer. Mrs. Gautal and Jeannie looked at each other but didn't say a word. Paul was feeling uncomfortable and was about to apologize when Annie bounced into the room happily. She stopped before the Canadian, kissed him and quickly sat down beside him.

"Good morning everyone," said Luisa who entered the room just after Annie.

Jeannie Donalt watched Luisa carefully and then asked:

"Do you feel well, Luisa?"

"As well as I'll ever feel," replied Luisa, somewhat nervously.

"The coffee this morning is a bit stronger than usual," said Mrs. Gautal apologetically, while placing the steaming pitcher in front of the Canadians.

"It doesn't really matter to me as I won't have any breakfast," said Luisa with a dismissive gesture.

Mrs. Gautal quickly turned towards Luisa to ask her:

"Not even eggs and bacon, Luisa?"

"No, Mrs. Gautal. Not even eggs and bacon can tempt me today; thanks," said Luisa in a harsh and uncharacteristic tone.

"The bacon is nice! Can I have yours too, Mom?" asked Annie while gobbling up the last of her slices.

Luisa watched the girl with a deep love reflected in her eyes.

"If you want, you can, honey," and turning towards the landlady she asked: "Mrs. Gautal, don't you think you should solve the rat problem once and for all? If they continue as they are ..."

Mrs. Gautal paused briefly from her task and facing Luisa, responded:

"You know, Luisa, I was thinking about a solution just a few days ago. Tomorrow morning I shall prepare a rat poison paste to deal with them."

***

That night, just after dinner had started, a comment from Paul Donalt darkened the room:

"Where's the bread being kept? It looks as if it was bitten by rats."

"Let me see," said Mrs. Gautal, taking the piece of bread in her hands.

"I apologize, I assure you that it will not happen again," blushed the landlady after verifying that the bread was indeed eaten at one end.

"Don't worry. This old fox likes jokes," said Jeannie, shocked by her husband's bluntness.

"I must worry. This is my business," said Mrs. Gautal and continued, "by the way, Alfred, could you get me some arsenic from the pharmacy so I can prepare some rat poison paste?"

"I'll try to, Mrs. Gautal. Although it's not that easy to get arsenic, I will do my best to satisfy your desire," responded Alfred.

After dinner, everyone adjourned, as usual, to the living room. Luisa Hayen and Mrs. Gautal stayed behind to tidy up. After everyone was gathered in the small lounge, Paul Donalt, addressing Annie, said:

"On that shelf up there, you'll find somebody waiting for you, my little friend."

Annie jumped up trying to get the box that she could see waiting on top of the cabinet.

"Will you help me? It's too high for me!"

"Put a chair in front of the cabinet and get it by yourself. Don't get into the habit of relying on other people to do everything for you," Alfred ordered the girl energetically.

Annie ran to get a chair. She placed in front of the cabinet, stretched out her arms, reached on top and grabbed the bulky package. She took a moment and then jumped down from the chair.

"I've got it! Now let's see what's inside," said the girl as if completely unaware of what was in the package. She opened it and with a big happy voice, exclaimed: "It's my doll! My new doll! Oh, how good you are Paul! I love you …" Annie said while jumped on his knees.

"Now there will have to be two dresses instead of one, because this lovely doll will have to wear one that's just like her owner," assured Luisa.

"Is it true that I'll get a new dress, Mom? What will the color be?" asked the girl with her little face filled with joy.

"It's true, darling. As for the color, you will have to choose it. Now, say good night to everyone and let's go to sleep! Tomorrow we'll be getting up very early; Good night everyone!" said Luisa as she took her daughter's hand and started to walk toward their bedrooms.

"Good night!" said Annie as she walked with her new doll hugging it sweetly to her cheek.

The night was long for Luisa, who struggled to fall asleep. The next day, she took Annie shopping. They bought a blue cloth and white ribbons for the new garments that she planned to sew for her daughter and for the new doll. Later, after they arrived back at the house, Luisa left Annie in her bedroom and went to the kitchen to help Mrs. Gautal prepare dinner. When the food was ready, they sat down to eat in the company of the other house guests.

The evening turned to be full of hope for the Hayens because, after dinner, while Luisa was stitching the blue cloth, Alfred made an announcement that gave everyone a reason for celebration:

"I've got a raise today!"

"Congratulations!" exclaimed Paul shaking his hand.

"Let it be for the good of your family!" wished Jeannie.

"Congratulations!" said Luisa.

"Will you buy a new pair of shoes to go with my blue dress, Alfred?" asked Annie euphorically.

"Of course, Annie," said Alfred as he turned the page of the book he was reading in between chats.

"We ought to buy some oranges to celebrate the event with freshly squeezed orange juice," proposed Mrs. Gautal a smile playing on her lips, adding after a short pause: "Oh, Alfred, did you get the arsenic that I asked you for?"

"That's not your problem anymore. I will prepare the rat poison tonight," said Alfred.

***

A week has passed since Luisa and little Annie returned to Mrs. Gautal's guest house. On the coffee table, the empty teacups were resting beside the half empty sugar bowl.

"What's going on lately with all the sugar in this house?" asked Mrs. Gautal collecting the tea service.

"I don't know," said Paul. "For days, after dinner, I've felt a bitter taste in my mouth. That's why I overload my tea with sugar, although, this doesn't happen only to me; Jeannie has the same problem. Today we consulted our doctor about it and he told us that it could be a malfunction of the liver."

"I'm sure it's not too serious," said Jeannie, "but in addition to the bitterness, I'm also suffering from digestive irregularities. At least, now I can say I have a better appetite. It's really weird. Don't you think?"

"Your appetite might have increased because of the cold season, since we tend to eat more in the winter and perhaps might also be due to the French wine we've been serving with meals since Luisa's return. But coincidentally, I also have a bitter taste in my mouth; I thought it might be due to too many cigarettes," said Alfred.

"It's not to say that you've got liver disease just for drinking a glass of wine at dinner time. On the contrary, some alcohol aids the daily functioning of the digestive system," said Mrs. Gautal.

"Perhaps you're right, Mrs. Gautal. I will try to cut down on smoking."

"We also ought to follow the good example, Paul," said Jeannie turning towards her husband.

"What's happening to all of you is that you're getting old. Look at me! Nothing wrong with me," interrupted Annie accompanying her ingenuous comment with a sweet smile. She then continued addressing her mother:

"When do you think I could wear my new dress, Mommy?"

"You may wear it on the day when Alfred gets his first raised salary. We will celebrate with a special dinner and we must dress nicely for the occasion," said Luisa.

"And how long do I have to wait until then, Alfred?" asked the girl turning to him.

"Seven days," said Alfred without taking his eyes from his book.

"Oh, I must remind you of something, before I forget again, Alfred. I need more arsenic to prepare more rat poison. Surely, Dr. Pamer would expect me to show him all the rats in the house before he would consent to write me another prescription," said Mrs. Gautal.

"And why would you need to buy more arsenic? There was enough of it leftover to prepare another mixture."

"Yes. You're right, there was indeed some leftover arsenic; but it's not where I left it anymore. It looks like someone played at housewives with it. I saw something that proves my theory in the dustbin," clarified Mrs. Gautal.

"But that's plain carelessness! These products should be kept safely where children live," exclaimed Luisa.

"Don't look at me! I didn't touch any of it!" said Annie as she shook her head vigorously.

"We all know it wasn't you, darling. To make sure this will not happen again, this time we will use the entire product," said Mrs. Gautal with a certain annoyance in her tone.

CHAPTER III

During the early December cold night, when it was previously agreed to celebrate Alfred's salary increase with a special dinner, Luisa helped Mrs. Gautal with serving the food. But the apparent harmony that prevailed in the atmosphere, could not erase the sour aftertaste of the previous night's discussions in which Luisa had threatened to leave the house especially for the sake of little Annie's physical safety. Moreover, the girl wanted a pet and it was made clear to her that such a fancy could not be indulged in a guesthouse.

Mrs. Gautal apologized at the time for any situation or event that could have put the safety of the child in danger and agreed for Annie to bring a pet to the house after all, practically begging Luisa to agree to continue her tenancy in her guesthouse.

Luisa's response was curt. She was determined to move and she would do as she pleased. Subsequently, she had to face Alfred's objections, which was quick to assure the landlady that they would not move from the guest house on a whim of his wife and without any serious consideration. Luisa lost it right then and there and railed against her husband and Mrs. Gautal, accusing them of having an intimate relationship behind her back. The landlady and her husband denied everything, belittling her. Luisa had no alternative but to prove her point by mentioning she overheard their little morning chat several days ago, stating that she was willing to apologize if Mrs. Gautal could offer any explanation for what she said that morning and if Alfred could somehow justify the reasons for her disastrous financial status.

Although several hours had passed since the quarrel and it was time for the celebration dinner, the atmosphere around the dinner table was still charged. Everyone was tense and defensive and the only person that seemed to not have been affected by any arguments was little Annie. Paul, who was trying to lighten up the ambiance, hoped that perhaps that dinner could bring accord and harmony to the guest house, making everyone forget their doubts and resentments. He tried to stay positive and praise everyone at every opportunity so, when seeing that Mrs. Gautal had placed the steaming tureen in the middle of the table, he immediately exclaimed:

"Yummy! That smells delicious! It looks like we're having very tasty soup, Mrs. Gautal."

"I've cooked it with love, Paul. I hope you're right."

"I'd like to inform you that apart from the increase in Alfred's salary, Paul and I are celebrating the official opening of our company," said Jeannie.

"Congratulations!" Alfred and Annie said in unison.

"I'm very happy for you," said Luisa.

"Well, well, well. At last I can know where my Canadian tenants work and what they do for a living," said Mrs. Gautal.

"Let's save the good news for the desert. That way we will have a nice topic of conversation," asked Luisa as she placed the fish dish on the table, adding: "I'll be back immediately with the wine and the jug of freshly squeezed orange juice that Mrs. Gautal just made. I'll be right back."

Dinner started with an appetizer of orange juice. It was followed by a green salad topped with blue cheese sauce and bread rolls topped with mayonnaise sauce. Then they enjoyed the mushroom soup followed by fish served by Mrs. Gautal, seasoned with juicy onion wheels and the chutney that Luisa had bought that afternoon on her way back from the bakery. For dessert, there was chocolate cake and apple jam. Everything was generously accompanied by the French wine that Luisa had brought from her trip to France.

"That was delicious!" said Paul rubbing his belly, then added: "I'm afraid I have no room left for any desserts."

"Ah! No, Paul. You can't leave me alone with that huge cake," objected Annie, while the others laughed at the child's remark.

After dinner, everyone was gathered in the small room as usual, enjoying an aromatic tea that the landlady served in her finest china, reserved for special occasions, when Annie observed:

"Everything was very tasty; but my stomach is burning. Could it be the orange juice?"

"It's possible, Annie. I also feel some discomfort but don't worry, we'll get better soon," said Paul, addressing the girl.

"I feel the same. Could it be the orange juice, as Annie believes?" argued Mrs. Gautal.

"Could be, but don't worry. I'm sure it will pass. We're just not used to drinking freshly squeezed orange juice," said Jeannie Donalt, downplaying the discomfort she also felt.

Luisa joined everyone in the living room, returning from her own room with a pack of cigarettes in her hands. She sat down and, holding out the package, handed it over to Alfred, saying:

"Excuse my short absence; I went to my room to get the Turkish cigarettes that I bought today for Alfred."

"Thanks, Louise! These are my favorites," said Alfred as he opened the package, took out a cigarette and lit it up.

The aromatic smell of Turkish tobacco captured everyone's attention for a moment. Then, Mrs. Gautal addressed Jeannie Donalt:

"And ... regarding your occupation Mrs. Donalt?"

"Ah! Sorry. I forgot I promised I will tell you all about it. We are sales agents for a company importing charcuterie. We had to maintain absolute discretion in order to avoid any mishaps with our competitors; but today all the problems have been solved; the documentation requested by the official media has been presented and we'll start working officially next week. Satisfied?" Jeannie said.

"But that's fantastic!" Mrs. Gautal said, turning to Paul, to ask:

"And what can you tell us about all this, Mr. Donalt?"

"That the dinner was delicious; but I have a lot of heartburn and I'm afraid I feel quite ill. Also, I feel a slight tightness in the chest and I'm struggling to breathe," answered Paul.

"Mommy, my stomach hurts! I'm going to throw up!" Annie cried, clutching her belly with both hands and vomiting.

Luisa ran to assist her daughter; but the same severe abdominal pain gripped her as well. She put both hands on her belly; she opened her eyes widely, vomited and collapsed on the floor; she was unconscious.

"Do something! Do something! They're going to die," shouted Jeannie in panic.

"Paul, go and get help immediately!" ordered Mrs. Gautal. "And you," she said addressing Jeannie Donalt, "help them however you can! I'll look for something to cover them up to keep them warm."

Paul ran downstairs. He also had a stomach ache and felt invaded by a terrible tiredness. His legs, usually light and always willing to travel long distances, weighed him down greatly, shaking. What could it be? Would it be the fish?

Through the fog he made out the police officer, patrolling the roundabout. He shouted as loudly as he could. The officer followed the direction the cry came from and approached the person; he stopped his bike and asked:

"Is there something wrong, sir?"

"Quickly!" said Paul. "There's no time to waste! Look for a vehicle to carry two seriously ill patients to the hospital! But don't waste any time, please. I'll wait for you at 113 Lombard Street."

***

The policeman arrived with the ambulance twenty minutes later. When he saw that no one was waiting for him, he thought that he'd been the victim of a practical joke or someone had wanted to distract him from his job. Only curiosity, when finding the door to the house open, brought him in and up the stairs. When he reached the living room, he was shocked. He could not believe his eyes. There, writhing on the floor apparently having severe seizures was the man who warned him earlier and five others, including a girl. He picked up the girl in his arms and hurried downstairs. He placed the fragile little body on the stretcher and ordered the driver:

"Take her to the hospital and send three more ambulances immediately! There are five more people in the same condition up there; this looks very serious. Hurry!"

The patient load had been so severe at the hospital that night that the doctors on duty failed to make the connection between the six people who recently arrived at the hospital suffering with the same unmistakable symptoms of choleric gastroenteritis. But the senior admissions doctor found it suspicious that all of them lived at the same address, but only two of them were in very serious condition; for this reason, he called the hospital director to discuss his suspicion that they might be dealing with a collective poisoning. Given his colleague's hypothesis, Dr. William Rust decided to visit the patients. He carefully studied the diagnosis and urgently ordered more laboratory tests to determine the causes of the phenomenon. Forty minutes later the lab report arrived at Dr. Rust's office:

To Dr. William Rust

The tests undertaken urgently, today December the 11th at 11:45 pm, for the patients in beds 15, 18, 19, 24, 27, and 29 of ward F, Pasteur building of this hospital, show the following results:

> *1) All are suffering from poisoning caused by ingestion of a toxin: Arsenic.*

> *2) They all have a similar amount of poison in their bodies, according to the investigation conducted in the laboratory of this center under the leadership of Dr. Boris Hull, who followed explicit instructions of Dr. William Rust, Director General of this centre and Dr. Roulf, doctor on duty.*

Dr. Boris Hull
Chief of Laboratory

Clutching the report, Dr. Rust turned and headed toward the room where the patients were resting. Upon arrival, Dr. Wensin greeted him with a questioning gesture. Dr. Rust handed him the results of the analysis by way of answer. He waited for his colleague to read the report and said:

"Your diagnosis was very accurate, Doctor Wensin. Now we shall see what we can do for them. Who is in worse condition?"

"The girl and one of the ladies are in very serious condition. They appear to be less resistant than the others to the toxin. The other four patients are also in serious condition, but they have reacted better. Especially the younger lady," answered Dr. Wensin.

"Now that we know what to expect, I'll leave everything in your hands. I'll call the extreme emergencies team to help you with your work. I will communicate with Scotland Yard. Keep me updated, please," said Dr. Rust as he left the room with the lab report in his hands.

CHAPTER IV

Just as dawn was breaking, a thin, medium height man, dressed in a black worn out suit stopped in front of the hospital director's office. He knocked on the door and heard Dr. Rust's answer: "Come in, please."

"Good morning, Sir. I hope I'm not inconveniencing you," said the newcomer while advancing towards Dr. Ruth with an outstretched hand and a slight hint of a smile, playing on his face.

"No problem, Inspector. I was waiting for you. Please take a seat."

"I'm sorry I couldn't come before, doctor, but it was quite impossible. Now, let's hear, what prompted you to call me night on my home number?"

"Well, Inspector, please accept my apologies for calling you at home, outside working hours," said Dr. Ruth. "Forgive my boldness, Inspector; but I wanted to make sure we could meet this morning. We have a suspicious case and I want you, to personally take a look at it."

"Thank you very much doctor; but don't worry, it wasn't such a big deal. Let's talk no more about it. What's going on?"

"Last night, we admitted six people into the emergency room, apparently suffering from choleric gastroenteritis, including a girl who's barely five years old. But on being admitted to the intensive care unit, judging by the patients' symptoms, Dr. Wensin suspected, more than an acute case of intoxication and decided to alert me as to his suspicions. After discussing it with him, I immediately called the laboratory for an urgent analysis and these are the result. Please read it!" said Dr. Rust as he extended the report to Inspector Fort.

The inspector read it carefully, while involuntarily stroking his jaw. After reading the document, he put it down, let out a sigh and sitting up as he stared at Dr. Rust, asked:

"After you've got this report, you called me immediately; am I right doctor?"

"Indeed, inspector."

"Well," said Inspector Fort sighing, "now I understand your concern and your call; but what did you do afterwards, doctor?"

"Doctor Wensin and I met with the hospital emergency team director in order to establish a plan that would at least give us hope of saving the life of anyone who could be saved. We started the treatment with a thorough gastric cleanse. Then we proceeded to deal with the patients' dehydration so we could apply an antidote to the toxic intravenously. Of course, not before ordering Dr. Hull to conduct an investigation to determine his most accurate estimate of the amount of arsenic in each of the patients' bloodstream."

"And what was the result, Dr. Rust?"

"It's most intriguing, inspector! The two patients who are on the verge of death are those that show less toxic in their system."

"As I understand, doctor, not all of us react the same way to certain poisons."

"You are correct! Not all organisms react in the same way; but it's rather suspicious that out of the six people affected, those that have the least amount of toxic substance in their blood are the ones that are almost dying. Don't you think, inspector?"

"It's very interesting, doctor. Do you have any explanation to this puzzle?"

"I have never liked guessing, inspector. I'm sorry that I cannot give you my opinion right away. I have to exchange views with Dr. Wensin before anything else, but I warn you, this does not seem to be an incidental fact."

"But what do you mean, doctor? Please explain."

"After, Inspector ... After I confirm my suspicions. Not before."

Finishing his sentence, Dr. Rust stood in farewell. Inspector Fort went away with a "See you later" through the corridor leading to the exit, where an official car with two detectives, was waiting for him. He got into the car and sat back. He took out a cigarette, lit it and took a long drag. He let out the smoke slowly and ordered the driver: 113 Lombard Street, please.

CHAPTER V

Inspector Fort's car was moving as fast as the surrounding fog and wet road allowed. It was intensely cold. The inspector was scanning the surroundings through the glass window when the car stopped in front of Mrs. Gautal's guest house. He opened the car door and stepped out as if compelled by an order. Briskly he walked to the front door, greeted the officer on duty and entered the building followed by Harold. The staircase was short. The furniture in the living room was untidy and the floor was covered in vomit. He crossed the room, trying not to destroy any evidence that could help the investigation later and ordered Harold to do the same. He walked down the corridor leading to the inner rooms, crossed the door leading to the dining room and stopped at the floor around the table. He noticed that it was clean. Harold called him at that moment to show him something suspicious in the kitchen. The dishes used the night before were clean, except for a tea set that was inside the sink which had not been cleaned. He searched through the rest of the room and saw a neatly folded table cloth on a little table. Under this table was the trash can. He unfolded the cloth and found several stains that appeared to be fruit juice or something similar. He put it aside and turned to inspect the trash can, looking for something that could lead to a clue. After rummaging through its contents, he put the lid on and said to his driver:

"Harold. Go to the lab and tell Dr. Richard Brook that I need his expertise here and now. See if he can come back with you, and please tell him to come properly prepared. Don't waste any time, please."

Inspector Fort was exchanging views with the residents of the guest house when Harold returned in his car.

"I came as fast as I could, Inspector said Dr. Brook in place of a greeting."

"Thank you, Richard. Let's get started as this will be a long day's work"

***

It was past midday when inspector Fort arrived at Dr. Rust's offices. The secretary rushed him immediately to the office, while she tried to locate the doctor who had gone to lunch a short time before.

Fifteen minutes of waiting were sufficient to see the figure of Dr. Rust appearing in the doorframe. His face revealed fatigue. He greeted inspector Fort affably and then said:

"I'm glad to see you, Inspector. I was going to call you to report the death of the child. In addition, I believe that the young woman, who according to the report is the child's mother, has only a few hours of life left."

Inspector Fort's face darkened. He didn't like it when children died. When he recovered, he said:

"Please, Dr. Rust, call forensics and have them perform the autopsy as soon as possible. I'll take care of the formalities and apply for permits."

"So be it' was Dr. Rust's answer. He paused a moment and added: Have you found any details that might help solve this case, Inspector?"

"That's very likely. We just have to wait for the results of the laboratory investigations. By the way, Dr. Rust, don't you think it's time I knew what your reckonings about this case are?"

"Well, I'll tell you. My colleagues and I believe that out of the six patients transferred to this hospital last night, four of them had been ingesting arsenic in small doses before. So their bodies adapted and developed a tolerance so that they could withstand a lethal dose. Of course, this kind of plan could doesn't need a long timeframe. The period of time a body needs in order to create a tolerance to a lethal dose ranges between ten and twenty days. Otherwise, the master mind of this plan, would have had to increase the dose to certain risky levels for the results to be unlike those of an ordinary choleric gastritis; an appearance that was almost achieved, if it wasn't for Dr. Wensin, who by having some experience in Toxicology, assumed that this was not a common disease."

"So that's why he was so astonished with the results shown by the blood tests, applied to each particular patient," guessed the inspector.

"Exactly, you'll be even more amazed when

you'll see the results of the autopsy. I suspect the girl's forensic results will show enough arsenic to validate our theory. What I can assure you, Inspector, is that this is one of the very few cases where the criminal used a tactic that is dangerous for its own life. There's no doubt that we're dealing with a crime, Inspector!"

***

The phone rang insistently. Inspector Fort walked to the phone with measured steps, due to the fatigue of an intense day of work.

"Who's there?"

"It's Dr. Wensin, inspector! Forgive me for bothering you, but Dr. Rust instructed me to call if the young woman died in your absence."

"How long since she died, Dr. Wensin?"

"Barely twenty minutes, inspector. I assure you I called you as soon as circumstances allowed me to."

"Thank you, Dr. Wensin. I appreciate it."

"Inspector, I have ordered the preparations for the autopsy," said the Dr. Wensin shyly.

"That's very thoughtful of you, Dr. Wensin. We act as we can. By the way, when will we be able to begin interrogations of the other residents of Lombard Street?"

"You still have to wait, inspector; but don't worry, when the time comes, we'll let you know."

"I trust you do, doctor. Now I must go to bed."

"Sleep well, inspector."

***

Just as dawn broke, the inspector and the forensic team were in the hospital, ready to begin their work. Everything had been arranged and organized in such a way that at half past eight in the morning, an employee of the Legal Laboratory would be ready to take the bodies of the deceased to the laboratory. The inspector waited for the forensics to change and drove them personally to their place of work. Once there, he went to the office and told the young secretary responsible for sending the department reports:

"Hello Betty. Did you send the Annie Banet autopsy report to my office?"

"We still don't have all the results, inspector; but I assure you when I get them, I will prepare a complete report that will reach your office immediately," said the secretary.

"Thank you, Betty. I trust you will," said the inspector, in farewell. He turned and headed out of the building.

When the car was moving, the inspector ordered Harold to go to Lombard Street. When the car stopped in front of the house marked 113, the policeman guarding the building came and opened the car door. On the sidewalk, the inspector, exchanged greetings with the officer, and asked:

"Is this neighborhood part of your usual route?"

"In is indeed, inspector!"

"What can you tell me about the inhabitants of this house?"

"They never gave us any trouble before."

"Do you know those who live here very well?"

"Not intimately, but enough to say that I can find no explanation to what happened."

"Who told you what happened, officer? Has the media reported this yet?" asked inspector Fort, raising his eyebrows.

"No one in particular, but all the neighbors say that it's poisoning because someone saw Mrs. Gautal buying arsenic in Dr. Diskan's pharmacy. Also they're gossiping that if it were a common disease, there wouldn't be a policeman always guarding the house, nor would you have bothered to come by so often."

"Where is that pharmacy, officer?" asked the inspector abruptly.

"Two blocks from here, inspector. If you wish, I can accompany you there," the constable said.

"Harold, please guard the house until we return," asked the inspector of his assistant.

"As you order, Inspector," said Harold, standing next to the entrance.

"I'll come with you, officer. Let's go to Doctor Diskan's pharmacy."

***

The next morning after meeting the night before and early morning hours with the pharmacist Dr. Diskan, the inspector's car headed to Dr. Carl Pamer's office, since he was the one who had issued the prescriptions which Mrs. Gautal and Alfred Hayen recently used to buy arsenic at the pharmacy.

The doctor was extremely terse in his responses. Evaluating every word and weighing every answer he gave, but his terse conversation was enough for the inspector. Dr. Pamer admitted that in reality he prescribed a preparation based on arsenic acid to a man who fitted the description of Alfred Hayen, and a few days later issued another prescription to a lady that corresponded to the description of Mrs. Gautal. On both occasions the prescriptions were issued at the customers' request and needed the product to prepare rat poison.

Back in his office, while inspector Fort was evaluating all the data in his possession, a call from the hospital arrived informing him that he could come in to question patients whenever he wished. This would certainly provide him with the opportunity to tie up some loose ends. He immediately picked up the autopsy results, from his desk. He made sure to have his notebook in his jacket pocket and went out to his car.

CHAPTER VI

Dr. William Rust, Dr. Wensin and Inspector Fort, were gathered in the office exchanging views about the mass poisoning that had occurred at 113 Lombard Street. They had been talking for more than an hour when Dr. Wensin made the following observation:

"I don't think, Inspector, there is any doubt as to who the real culprits are."

"We mustn't assume anything, Dr. Wensin, since we're still waiting for the results of the interrogations," clarified Dr. Rust.

"If we look at the facts analytically, I believe that my conversation with them will provide data that will help corroborate my theory," said the inspector.

"I agree with you, but I never allow myself to judge by appearances," said Dr. Rust sententiously.

"I'm not judging by appearances. It's just that everything points towards them," said the inspector.

"I reiterate your thesis, inspector," said Dr. Wensin, adding after a brief reflection: "If it was not them, who was it? The Canadians show no apparent reason to be suspects. Don't you think so, Doctor Rust?"

"Your reasoning is not without logic, Doctor Wensin, but you can't rule them out as possible perpetrators yet," said Dr. Rust.

"May I remind you that I'm waiting for you to take me to them? The sooner I begin these preliminary investigations, the better," said the inspector addressing the doctors.

"I'd advise you to be tactful, inspector. They were all in critical condition until a few hours ago. Remember, inspector, to be gentle especially with the Canadian girl," advised Dr. Wensin.

"Don't worry, Doctor Wensin, I will work with tact and caution," said the inspector determined to follow the doctor's instructions.

The patients' beds were strategically separated to facilitate the inspector's interrogation, so when Inspector Fort and the doctors who accompanied him came into the room, all eyes turned toward them. The inspector asked doctor Wensin something softly, to which he responded:

"Start with the Canadian so she doesn't get anxious and be as prudent as possible, I beg you, inspector. She has been in a very serious condition."

"Rest assured that nothing will happen. In addition, it's her for who I have the least questions since apparently the death of the child and her mother brought her nothing but grief," the inspector clarified.

"I agree with you again, inspector," said Dr. Wensin, "because since she regained consciousness she asks with a maddening constancy for the child. So if you can avoid letting her know of the death of the little girl, I would ask you to do so."

"I'm afraid I can't do so, doctor. Undoubtedly, the death of the child is the only thing that could break the reservations that some of these people might have with respect to what has been going on daily in the guest house."

"Go ahead then, inspector, let's talk to Jeannie Donalt."

Inspector Fort followed the doctor with a firm step towards the place where Mrs. Donalt's bed was. The young woman was visibly alarmed by the conversation the two men held in connection with her. Because without a doubt it was about her, they talked about since as they walked, they pointed to the part of the room where her bed was and nothing else. Dr. Wensin noticed her anxiety and pleasantly approached her bed saying:

"I see you're a lot better. I hope you are willing to talk to this gentleman; he has a few questions to ask you. Don't be alarmed, because although I'm sure you have never found yourself in a similar situation, I can assure you that if you did, you could not have encountered a kinder and more considerate person than Inspector Fort."

"Inspector Fort! I wonder what the police want with me. What sort of questions do you mean, doctor? What happened? Please explain!" asked Jeannie anxiously.

"I'll be the one to explain it all Mrs. Donalt, since

Dr. Wensin has done enough with introducing us. Now he must retire to attend to his work. Is that not true, doctor?" asked the inspector so that the doctor realizes that he wishes to be left alone with the patient.

"Oh yes! See you soon and remember to be as gentle as possible," said Doctor Wensin as he walked over to where Doctor Rust was waiting.

Once alone with Inspector Fort, Mrs. Donalt asked:

"What did he mean when he said that you ought to be as gentle as possible?"

"It's very difficult to say; but I'll try to be as explicit as I can, provided that you'll give me your full cooperation."

"Count on it," assured Jeannie somewhat calmer.

"Well, let's see. A few nights ago, the phone rang insistently in my house. When I answered, it was the director of this hospital asking me to come in person to his office as soon as I could..."

When the Inspector Fort finished the events of what happened that night until the present, Jeannie did nothing but to shake her head and repeat:

"Why her? Why did she have to die and not me? Why her? Why?"

Due to the impact that the news of Annie's death had on the patient, the inspector had to wait until she regained her composer before he could begin questioning. Once Jeannie was a bit more serene, he asked the first question:

"What do you think of all this, Mrs. Donalt?"

"I don't know, inspector. I can't think of any explanation. It's simply horrible." The woman paused, thoughtfully, and then added: "and to think I considered her a decent woman of good feelings."

"Who do you mean?"

"Who else do you think I mean, if not Mrs. Gautal?"

"What do you base your suspicions on?"

"Huh? What are my grounds to suspect her, you ask Inspector? Perhaps you can tell me who, if not she alone, could have done it? Who had more reasons than anyone else to commit a crime so she can get what she wanted? Who else directly linked to the kitchen could have prepared such a horrible and complicated death as this?"

"Then you suspect Mrs. Gautal as the author of the crime?" asked the inspector.

"Yes!" replied Jeannie dryly to the question.

"Do you know the weight your testimony would have against Mrs. Gautal and the responsibility that would fall on your shoulders if you are not correct in your suspicions?"

"Yes, I know. But I'm not afraid, because I'm sure she's guilty," Jeannie stressed firmly.

"Calm down, Mrs. Donalt, stay calm and try to think things through. What I want from you is an impartial opinion, not a verdict. For example, tell me more about Mrs. Luisa Hayen and if you can, give me your opinion about why she could have been targeted by a murderer."

Silence reigned for a few minutes, and then Jeannie said in a compassionate tone:

"Mrs. Luisa Hayen was one of those people for whom life reserves the worst. After an unhappy and unsettled childhood, according to what she had told me, she married a traveler of some sort who brought her with him to London. Things seemed to have worked out well for her but this happiness was cut short by her husband's death, occurring four years later. The result of this marriage was little Annie. Some time later, Luisa married Alfred Hayen, initially recommended to be the manager for her inherited estate; as a result of his bad investments, they lost everything and had to sell their house. That's when the Hayen family moved into Mrs. Gautal's guest house. There was no one nobler and kinder than Luisa. Nobody cared for others more than her. She was always smiling and willing to sacrifice herself for others happiness. Only once I remember seeing her angry and it was just the night before the facts."

"Tell me more about this event, please," asked the inspector.

"I will. It was on the night of December the 10th. We were all in the living room drinking tea and enjoying the usual after dinner chat when Luisa informed us that she was planning to move out of the guest house. After arguing that her decision was based on the fact that it was inadequate for a child to live there, Annie, stood in the middle of the room, overhearing the conversation. Not knowing in reality it was not over her that they were planning to leave, but because her mother was very jealous of Mrs. Gautal. This started a brief but sharp exchange between Alfred and Louise which was very uncomfortable for us to hear. Finally, they agreed to continue the discussion in private.

After this, a very uncomfortable calmness settled over the room as this event ensued."

"Now please tell me about Annie Bannet," asked the inspector.

"I can't believe she's dead. She was so kind, lively and noble, so affectionate and nice. Very rare were the nights when she didn't make us laugh out loud. I assure you, Inspector, that Paul felt like she was his own daughter. She went on to win his affection and love. To the extent, that my husband came to confess, after the dispute, that if Annie moved out, we should move out too because he could not live without the girl beside him."

"Tell me about the relationship between the child and her stepfather, please," asked the inspector calmly.

"It was generally good. Only Alfred constantly admonished her because he said the girl fantasized too much," replied Jeannie, as she furtively wiped away a tear.

"Mrs. Donalt, what can you tells me of the relationship between Mrs. Gautal and the child?" asked the inspector.

"These were more bad than good. Mrs. Gautal felt an aversion for the girl, because she had accused her, repeatedly, of kissing Alfred. In addition, she restricted her sugar and didn't allow the girl to bring her yellow cat into the house which was the girl's weakness," said Jeannie.

"We should understand then, that by these very particular criteria, the only people with apparent reasons for having committed the crime were Mrs. Gautal and Mr. Alfred Hayen," suggested Inspector Fort staring into the Canadian's eyes.

"Yes, inspector," said Jeannie.

"Let's see, Mrs. Donalt. Did you notice any suspicious behavior between them during the days leading up to the facts?" The inspector asked.

"Not really. I didn't notice anything special or unusual in their attitudes," replied Jeannie.

"Now concentrate, Mrs. Donald," pleaded the inspector. "According to our suspicions, the arsenic was given to you in daily doses. The murderer did it during dinner, since you and your husband's jobs did not allow you to have lunch at the guest house. Do you remember if prior to 11th of December you noticed any unusual or strange taste in the food or if any of the foods gave you an unpleasant feeling when ingested?"

"Now that I come to think of it, yes and I even consulted a doctor who said it could be due to a liver disease caused by ingestion of some foods," said Jeannie.

"Would it be possible to remember which foods had an odd taste? Make an effort, please," asked the inspector.

"It would be a wasted effort; lately everything tasted odd," said Jeannie.

"All right, Mrs. Donalt. Now think carefully before answering," requested the inspector. "Was the dinnerware placed on the table immediately before serving dinner or had Mrs. Gautal placed it on the table in advance?"

"The service was placed before serving dinner. No doubt about that," said Jeannie.

"Were the foods served in separate dishes?" asked the inspector.

"Yes, in separate dishes. As is the custom in most guest houses," said Jeannie.

"So there's no possibility of thinking that the dishes could have been used as a means to provide you with your daily ration of arsenic," said the inspector.

"Not really. Such a possibility is not logical. In addition, Luisa and I took turns to help Mrs. Gautal with placing the dishes on the table. As for the juice, I'd say that on that night was something exceptional, in honor of Alfred's salary increase. What we used to drink was a refreshing drink with orange flavor," said Jeannie.

"What salary increase?" asked the puzzled inspector?

"Well, you see, inspector. The company, for which Mr. Hayen worked, gave him a raise. So Mrs. Gautal decided to offer a special dinner in honor of the event, on the day her tenant should receive his first increased paycheck. That is why on the evening of December the 11th we were offered a dinner of creamed potatoes, fish, green salad covered with a cream cheese and mayonnaise sauce, applesauce, chocolate cake, bread and butter; quite a banquet. In addition, Mrs. Gautal asked Mr. Hayen to buy fresh oranges from the market for juicing them and serve the juice as an appetizer, replacing the usual squash, which didn't please Luisa or Annie."

"Do you mean to say that neither Mrs. Luisa Hayen, nor Annie drank the orange squash?" The inspector wanted to know with a strange gleam in his eyes.

"No. They never drank it," said

Jeannie.

"Was this refreshment served every day?" The inspector asked.

"Yes. That was the custom."

"Then the idea of natural orange juice was to give the mother and daughter a chance to share the drink that was being served that evening," demanded the inspector.

"So it was, inspector. That was the purpose."

"Mrs. Donalt, please make an effort to remember," the inspector said. "Did you notice any strange taste in the orange juice?"

"In all honesty, I have to admit that the taste was not normal; but I thought it was due to the fact I wasn't used to it," said Jeannie.

"Did anyone else besides you, noticed the weird taste?"

"Yes. Annie and Paul," she replied.

"That's enough. Finally, I think I know how you were supplied a daily dose of arsenic, without the mother and child having a share and without anyone realizing it," said Inspector Fort, with a hint of triumph in his voice.

"Do you mean that we were supplied this dose with the orange squash because the mother and daughter didn't drink it?" Jeannie wondered.

"This is apparently what happened. So thank you very much and forgive me for the inconvenience this conversation may have caused to you. You have been very cooperative Mrs. Donalt."

***

Inspector Fort sat next to Paul Donalt. He smiled and then said:

"Maybe you've wondered why I had such a long and private conversation with your wife, but I'm sure that, as soon as I explain the reasons that brought me here, you will also offer to help me. Listen to me and I urge you to be strong, because what I have to tell you may not be to your liking."

When the inspector finished relating to Mr. Donalt what happened to Mrs. Hayen and her daughter, plus the doctors' opinion regarding building arsenic tolerance through ingestion of small doses of the poison and the results of all tests performed in laboratories, Paul said in a voice that betrayed his emotion:

"After the death of my mother, this is the hardest blow I have ever received. Count on me for whatever you may need, inspector!"

There was a pause in the conversation. The inspector would have a great ally. He knew how much Paul loved the girl and what she meant to the Canadian, so he hoped Mr. Donalt would share every detail, however small it might be, that could help do her justice. Paul Donalt stared at the inspector, and clearing his throat, said:

"Inspector you can start. Tell me what you need to know."

"Mr. Donalt, please without allowing yourself to be carried away by emotion, tells me your opinion about the events of the night of 11th of December at Mrs. Gautal's guest house."

The Canadian closed his eyes perhaps looking for absolute concentration in order to answer with the utmost precision to the inspector's question. After several minutes had passed, he slowly opened his eyes, stared at the inspector and said:

"There are only two people on whom my suspicions fall, Inspector. One is Alfred Hayen and the other is Mrs. Gautal as for Jeannie I am confident that she's trustworthy."

"What are the reasons that lead you to that conclusion, Mr. Donalt?" inquired the inspector controlling the tone of his voice.

"Several, Inspector, several; but we'd understand each other better if we spoke of each separately. Agree?" asked Paul.

"As you think most fit, Mr. Donalt," said the inspector as he sought comfort in the metal chair on which he sat.

"We shall start then with Mrs. Gautal. This lady, as you are already informed, is the owner of the guest house in which we live. She acquired a legacy from her late husband, as she told us. She performs all duties of the guesthouse. She cooks and cleans the premises, which means that in order to increase her profits she doesn't mind that she can easily pass as a maid. However, she makes concessions to the ladies living under her roof and wishing to lend some assistance with the chores, especially in the kitchen. At first glance, Mrs. Gautal seems a respectable lady, but according to some gossip, there are those who suspect her of having led a depraved life during the time she was married to Robert Gautal and now there's some gossip that she is having an intimate affair with Alfred Hayen. This could be one of the motives for the murder although one could say that she may have served as an instrument for the true murderer."

"Please, Mr. Donalt, can you clarify this?"

"You see Inspector; since the day I met Alfred Hayen, I distrusted him. I suspected that his reputation was not good; hence I started doing some research that confirmed my suspicions. Later, I wondered about the reasons that led him to marry Luisa, because although he seems solicitous and attentive to her, it was obvious that the marriage was to him a mere business relationship. So, when I was informed of the reasons that had led him to take that step, I thought that a man of his class would seek a quick solution to get rid of these matrimonial ties, which he didn't need. A solution that should be carefully prepared, because if Luisa imagined that he intended to leave her, she could present him with a lawsuit for embezzlement and misuse of property that he had administered for her and for little Annie. This would have led him straight to jail, there's no doubt about it. So, when I realized that the relations with Mr. Hayen were suspicious, I thought he simply had a plan to get rid of his wife, but I never imagined that Alfred's wickedness went as far as murder, let alone that Annie was to be a victim."

At mentioning the name of the girl and facing the reality of her death, Paul was speechless. The inspector waited a few seconds and when it was deemed prudent, said:

"Mr. Donalt. Your words make me think you've been anticipating the catastrophic events that led to Mrs. Hayen and her daughter's death."

"Perhaps, inspector, perhaps, because although it's true that her circumstances were very influential, so it is also a fact that I don't have children of my own and know that my wife is unable to have children," said Paul.

"Let's recap, Mr. Donalt, let's recap," continued Inspector Fort. "According to your speculations, Mrs. Gautal was the direct instrument or the murderous hand, because it was easier to perpetrate a crime that would leave both free of suspicion while Mr. Hayen as being the criminal mastermind who devised, organized and ordered how to carry it out. Do we agree?"

"In fact, these are my conclusions," replied the Canadian.

"Mr. Donalt", Inspector Fort said slowly, "since you're a person who doesn't miss any details, would it be possible to tell me, whether you have any knowledge about where or how Mr. Hayen could have obtained the necessary knowledge that enabled him to plan and execute a crime that required some mastery of medical science?" inquired the inspector.

"From the moment you said Mrs. Hayen and Annie died as a result of arsenic poisoning and that we too had been poisoned, but survived because our bodies were prepared beforehand to tolerate a lethal dose of arsenic, I was even more convinced that my suspicions had always been well placed."

"Please, Mr. Donalt, be more accurate," the inspector prompted.

"Excuse me inspector, I'll try to be more precise. Now listen carefully: The day we found ourselves here, I had a clear sense of things, that is, I was not as bad as Jeannie, but I had severe headaches and my liver hurt at the slightest touch. So, as soon as I had an opportunity to talk with the nurse who assisted us, I asked about the cause of hospital admission that kept all of us, residents of the guest house, in the hospital beds. What was my surprise when I was informed that we had been victims of collective poisoning; Mr. Hayen, Mrs. Gautal and the rats immediately came to my mind?"

"Give me more details about this, Mr. Donalt. I'm listening carefully," said Inspector Fort as he tried to sit comfortably in the metal chair.

"Mrs. Gautal's guest house is infested with rats," began the Canadian, "so much so that foods that are not properly stored get nibbled by rodents and sometimes, when they find nothing, they venture up to the bedrooms. It was for this reason that one morning Mrs. Hayen asked Mrs. Gautal to do something about it. Later that day, at dinner, I found a piece of bread bitten by rats and I mentioned it. Mrs. Gautal asked Alfred to urgently bring her some arsenic from the pharmacy. Alfred brought it and prepared rat poison in which he used half of the arsenic. The other half was kept to repeat the process if necessary. At first many rats died and the stench filled the house, to the point of being unbearable to stay there. Then there was a little break, because the rat poison was almost gone and the rest remained in the cans uneaten. So as not to allow them to return, Alfred prepared more rat poison paste, following Mrs. Gautal's advice, with a similar amount of arsenic he had bought the first time, so as not to risk the remainder going astray, as had happened on a previous occasion."

"Give me more details on what was wasted, Mr. Donalt," interrupted the inspector.

"It happened this way," the Canadian began saying. "From the first amount of arsenic that was supposed to be used in the preparation of rat poison, Alfred took about half, giving the rest to Mrs. Gautal to save for the subsequent preparation of a new mixture; but when Mrs. Gautal was about to use it, she could not find it. As hard as she looked, she couldn't find it and could only conclude that the little girl had taken it to play with, since in the previous days she had seen food scraps mixed with a white powder in the trash can. That was why Mrs. Gautal bought additional arsenic and used it all to prepare more rat poison, which, to everyone's amazement, didn't have any effect!"

"How can it be possible that the rat poison containing twice the amount of arsenic did not have any effect? I will order a new analysis today," decided Inspector Fort, adding: "Don't stop, but if you know, enlighten me as to how come Alfred Hayen had the necessary knowledge to use the arsenic."

"Listen inspector!" the Canadian said as he watched Inspector Fort tried to make him comfortable in the metal chair. "At night, after dinner, everyone gathered in the living room for a chat. Alfred, meanwhile, listened to the radio quietly, smoking one cigarette after another and between conversations; he kept glancing at a large book with a worn out cover. My curiosity was stronger than my prudence and therefore one fine day, I ventured to ask Mr. Hayen about the type of content in that book that fascinated him so. He said that it was a book that the former owners of the building had left behind, a treaty of Pharmacology about the use of toxic products as stimulants. As I told him that in recent days, I had been hearing about this matter, he began to explain, in detail, about the use of strychnine and some other toxins, and lethal substances used in pharmacy without any risk to those who consume them if it is are well managed. I wish I had had the hindsight to be able to guess that such a book would be an effective instrument in a devious crime."

"Do you know if that book also discusses the use of arsenic, Mr. Donalt?" asked Inspector Fort.

"Indeed, Inspector," replied the Canadian. "That book contains information about the use of arsenic as a sexual stimulant and refers to some residents of certain Italian and Austrian villages, who ingest arsenic and enjoy excellent health."

"That makes you believe that this book is the source of Alfred Hayen's knowledge about the use of arsenic?"

"There's no doubt about it, is there?" The Canadian asked rhetorically.

Inspector Fort abruptly stood up, held out his hand to Paul in farewell and said:

"Thank you, Mr. Donalt. You have provided me with valuable information that could be decisive in this case. I'll see you again if I need you. Ah! I forgot. I must inform you that neither you nor your wife can leave London, without prior authorization." Inspector Fort was leaving when Paul said:

"Inspector, would you do me a favor if it's not too inconvenient for you?"

"What's the favor, Mr. Donalt?"

"Will you tell me where Annie's grave is? I would love to take her flowers."

CHAPTER VII

Alfred Hayen was in his bed, reclining on pillows. The Inspector Fort took a chair, greeted him and sat down in front of the patient close enough to be able to perceive the slightest changes in the intensity of his breathing. Alfred Hayen, meanwhile, looked up with some curiosity, and then wondered who this man might be and what had he been talking about with the Canadians. He looked genuinely intrigued about the topic of the conversation between them and about his motives for being there. Would it be the police? He found himself musing on this, when the inspector woke him from his pensiveness by saying;

"Mr. Alfred Hayen, would it be too inconvenient if I'd ask you a few questions?"

"No. I won't have any problem answering; but whom do I have the pleasure of talking to?" asked Alfred.

"Oh! Excuse my carelessness. I'm Inspector Joe Fort, from Scotland Yard Criminal Squad."

"Scotland Yard! What have I got to do with Scotland Yard?" asked Alfred.

"Mr. Hayen. Do you know the reason why you're being held in this center?"

"Oh! Of course! Due to some sort of food intoxication," he said.

"Do you know the causes of this intoxication?"

"I don't. I have no idea. Maybe it was the fish we had for dinner."

"You're not very inquisitive Mr. Hayen," said the inspector with suspicion in his voice.

"Just trying not to be a nuisance to others by asking unnecessary questions," muttered Alfred.

"Not even when your own health is in danger?"

"Not even!"

"Well then, I am informing you that you are being hospitalized as a consequence of poisoning by ingestion of arsenic," said the inspector.

"Poisoning by arsenic?" Alfred repeated appearing not to believe his ears.

"Yes, with arsenic. Mr. Hayen."

"But how was that possible?"

"I don't think I am the right person to answer that question," said the inspector.

"Who is it then?" asked Alfred, with true signs of unease.

"Calm down, Mr. Hayen suggested the inspector. Try to stay objective and let's talk frankly, perhaps this way we can clarify many things."

"From what I can gather, this is an interrogation."

"No. It's just a statement that will help me with the case I'm currently working on. Of course, if you are involved, all we discuss today will become part of your statement. However, if you wish I can leave now and wait for you in my office when you can come and talk to me while being accompanied by your lawyer, as the law provides," clarified Inspector Fort.

"I don't need to hire a lawyer, inspector. If you'd like to talk, let's talk. I have nothing to hide; but before we continue, please tell me, what case brings you here? What is the crime? Who committed it?" asked Alfred.

"You see, Mr. Hayen. The case I refer to is the one that has been opened in connection with the events in the guest house located at 113 Lombard Street, on the night of 11th of December. The apparent crime is collective poisoning, which caused the death of Mrs. Luisa Hayen and her daughter Annie Bannet as for your last question I can't answer because, we're only just started the investigative process," said the inspector.

Upon hearing Inspector Fort's words, Alfred Hayen's face contorted. The inspector, staring at him immediately told him:

"Don't tell me that you didn't find it strange not to see them in this hospital room, along with the other residents of the house. Is it you're really not that curious about the only two people that are directly related to you, Mr. Hayen?"

Alfred's face was in dismay. He was still unable to coordinate his thoughts in order to face the reality that was slowly dawning upon him. He was stupefied fixing his sight on the bottom rail of his hospital bed. Inspector Fort didn't waste time while watching askance at Mrs. Mary Gautal, who tried to hide the shock suffered after hearing what she heard. Suddenly, inspector Fort launched a torrent of questions towards Alfred Hayen.

"Tell me, Mr. Hayen. What motivated you to marry Luisa Hayen? How would you define the relationship with your wife and your stepdaughter? Where is the fortune bequeathed by Mr. Orson Bannet to his wife and daughter, whom you administered, first as an absolute representative of all the widow's assets and later as her husband?"

The avalanche of questions thrown by the Inspector Fort woke Alfred from his aloofness so, turning his gaze towards the window, he said:

"I'm sorry, inspector. I'm very sorry. I can't continue this conversation. The impact you're having on me is very intense. Please come back another day or, if you want, wait until I can leave the hospital and I'll come to your office. Do what you see fit but please kindly leave now. I am not in a position to continue this conversation."

Inspector Fort stood up. Without taking his eyes off the patient he rolled back the metal chair in which he sat during the interview; he clenched the small notepad tightly in his hand the small notepad and said softly to the patient:

"I'll talk to you again soon, Mr. Hayen. See you next time."

***

Mrs. Mary Gautal tried to hide the emotion that overwhelmed her, after hearing the few words she had managed to capture from the conversation between Alfred and the man who was now headed towards her bed. She imagined the fate suffered by Luisa Hayen and little Annie; but the confirmation of her suspicions impressed her greatly. She intended to ask the nurses in the room about the girl and her mother; but she restrained herself, fearing the man knew she had overheard their conversation while he spoke to Alfred. Suddenly a shiver went down her spine when she saw Inspector Joe Fort stop beside her bed. She took a deep breath, trying to appear calm and asked:

"What can I help you with, sir?"

"I'd like, if you don't mind to answer some questions for me," said the inspector.

"I'm a little tense, you know; but I will make an effort to please you."

"Thank you, Mrs. Gautal."

"I see you know my name, but I haven't gotten the pleasure of knowing yours."

"Oh! Excuse my manners for not introducing myself; I'm Inspector Joe Fort from Scotland Yard."

"Are you from Scotland Yard?"

"Indeed, Scotland Yard," stressed the inspector.

"I don't understand. I don't know what interest you can possibly have in talking to me," said Mrs. Gautal.

"About the events occurred in your house on the night of Dec. 11th."

"What events?" Mrs. Gautal asked.

"Multiple poisoning," said the inspector.

"Multiple poisoning you says!"

"Did you know about the death of Mrs. Luisa Hayen and that of her daughter Annie?"

"I only just overheard it when you told Mr. Hayen."

"Did you manage to hear what was the cause that led them to their death?" asked the inspector.

"No, I didn't," said Mrs. Gautal.

"Well, we suspect they died from poisoning, Mrs. Gautal."

"Poisoning!" exclaimed Mrs. Gautal.

"Yes. What's interesting in this case is that the rest of the inhabitants of the house, including you, suffered a similar poisoning that did not cause death. It's as if someone had hatched a devious plan aimed at getting rid of only Mrs. Hayen and her daughter Annie," replied the inspector.

"Are you insinuating that we're talking about murder?"

"It's possible."

"Do you have a suspect already?"

"Yes. You are all suspects."

"Including me?" she asked alarmed.

"I'm afraid so. Reasons abound for harboring

suspicions against you, since it's precisely you who was in charge of preparing food in the guesthouse," said the inspector.

"Why do you accuse me? On what are you basing your accusations?"

"Try to stay calm Mrs. Gautal. Gather all your strength and objectively tell me all about the animosity that existed between you, Mrs. Luisa Hayen and little Annie."

"There wasn't any animosity between us. It was a mere incompatibility of personalities that caused us to argue from time to time. Everyone has witnessed how she and I shared domestic chores and my efforts to earn the affections of little Annie," stressed Mrs. Gautal.

"How would you define your relationship with Alfred Hayen?" asked the inspector.

"You're being rude and impertinent! Get out of my sight or I call the nurse to throw you out immediately!" exclaimed Mrs. Gautal angrily.

"Don't worry Mrs. Gautal. I know exactly the way to out," Inspector Joe Fort said in farewell, as he rolled back in the metal chair and got up to leave.

CHAPTER VIII

Just a few moments earlier, Dr. Ernest Lesser understood why the London press gave him so little chance of success in the case he was about to defend. Precisely this morning, he had read a comment concerning the murder case at 113 Lombard Street, which had filled him with rage. The article revered the extensive experience, knowledge of the law and skill in performance in court of Sir Ralf Wilcot, a lawyer who was acting as the prosecutor for the case. So the press was already forecasting that soon enough the prosecutor would have an advantage over his inept opponent, an inexperienced lawyer who simply wouldn't stand a chance. Ernest Lesser reluctantly admitted that his opponent was considered the best lawyer in England. On the other hand, he understood the enormous benefit of facing a celebrity like Sir Ralf Wilcot at this point in his career and what it would bring him if he won. Suddenly he felt intimidated, petrified and rather cornered by the case presentation Sir Ralf Wilcot had made. He simply could not think of a way to start to cope with this unexpected situation. He used to consider himself ready to fight any strategy that the prosecution might use and was now bewildered by how much he underestimated the current situation. He was facing Inspector Fort and didn't know where to begin. The jury was visibly impressed by the way the prosecutor presented the case. Ernest Lesser looked askance at his opponent, looking for some detail that would regain his confidence; while the prosecutor covertly watched his moves with a slight smile on his face.

'Where shall I start?' Lesser thought again. He stroked his chin and constructed a mental picture of the presentation that Sir Ralf Wilcot would make at the beginning of the process, seeking a gap to channel his interrogation of Inspector Fort. The prosecutor had been very brief at his first opportunity to speak in the trial; he merely informed the court about the life of the accused. He began talking about the disregards for morality led by Mary Gautal during led her life, while still married to her late husband Robert Gautal. Immediately he hinted at her husband's strange death - sudden stroke, according to medical reports at the time. One could involuntarily be led to think, it's one of the many ways of viewing a crime of poisoning appear as a natural death, given the similarity of this disease with the effects of certain toxics.

It was at that moment that he objected and addressed Dr. David Rogell, who had been appointed as the judge for the case, for the insinuations of his opponent, regarding the death of the accused's husband. The objection was accepted, but was ineffective because of the doubt that had already been thrown to the jury. Sir Ralf Wilcot continued his presentation. He referred to the conditions that prompted the Hayen family to take residence at 113 Lombard Street and the alleged intimate relations between the two defendants, as stated by the other house guests. He stressed Alfred Hayen's haphazard life. Starting with his childhood, and disorderly adolescence, without forgetting to describe the slum where the accused grew up. Also, the time that Alfred Hayen had served in the army and participated in the war which went almost unnoticed; but he was quick to emphasize the way Alfred had contacted Mrs. Luisa Lonfard, whom he married after squandering her estate through dubious mismanagement, and as accused, poisoned her in an attempt to avoid a judicial inquiry that would have sent him to prison.

Once again the defense lawyer objected to the prosecutor's argument before but this time the judge had overruled the objection, arguing that the prosecutor was still within the boundaries of the case. Then he realized how much advantage Sir Ralf Wilcot had gained in just a few minutes, and how hard he had to work if he wanted to take the lead; but who would have thought that Sir Ralf Wilcot's case presentation would also make reference to the causes of death of Robert Gautal. This unusual method, used by the prosecutor led to requesting the appearance of Inspector Joe Fort from the Criminal Brigade Scotland Yard, as the first prosecution witness, which took even Dr. Rogell by surprise.

The inspector was thorough and extremely careful when listing the facts. He started with the phone call that notified him of the case on the night of 11 December, which led him to an interview with Dr. Rust. He then explicitly stated the research method, the tests performed in the legal laboratory and everything else concerning the case of which he had full knowledge. It was all that had happened until then. Now, it was up to him to take advantage of the inspector's future responses; but how? Suddenly, he had a brilliant idea so, without even thinking, he asked the question:

"Inspector Fort. I'd like to know your thoughts about the motive for the crime my clients are accused of. I believe that everyone deserves to know your views on this matter, as I consider it the basis of the whole case."

Where did he get the idea for such a question, he didn't know for sure, but he clearly noticed that the jurors, at hearing what he had just asked, shifted uneasily in their seats, waiting for new revelations that would be significant. However, despite knowing that he had touched the only point on which could base the defense, his concerns were increasing, especially when glancing towards Sir Ralf Wilcot and seeing that smile further reaffirmed on his face.

"There seems to be several motives," Inspector Joe Fort began speaking. "If I may, I will start with the motives that according to my research may have prompted Mr. Alfred Hayen to commit the crime. In the first instance, it appears that Mr. Alfred Hayen married Mrs. Luisa Lonfard, widow of Bannet, motivated by her wealth and seeking to prevent Mrs. Lonfard starting a judicial inquiry into the mismanagement of her estate, when she realized that the estate administered by Alfred Hayen was disappearing. Secondly, he would regain his independence and with it, the cessation of his responsibilities as a husband. Thirdly, he couldn't give his wife a reasonable explanation about his relationship he had with the landlady. All this can be summed up as a motive for his personal safety. As for the motives that prompted Mrs. Mary Gautal to collaborate in carrying out the crime, well... everything seems to indicate that she was seeking Mr. Alfred Hayen's security and independence. Obviously this is based on the alleged romance between them, according to some statements. As for the causes that prompted them to kill the child as well as the mother, you can say that it was for security reasons, because with Luisa's daughter out of the game, it was very unlikely that anyone would ever show any interest in opening an investigation regarding the estate she had inherited from her father."

"Inspector Fort," Dr. Ernest Lesser interrupted. "What you have just told us, regarding the possible motives that led the accused to commit the alleged crime, is based on your case investigation, am I right?"

"Yes, that's correct," replied the inspector.

"Inspector Fort," said Dr Lesser, now more confidently, "It's a fact that the supposed reasons that may have prompted Mr. Alfred Hayen to commit the murder, are reflected in accounting books and bank accounts that have been collected and analyzed; but is there any reliable proof that an inappropriate relationship between the two defendants exists or existed?"

Mr. Ernest Lesser was sure that he had just dealt a sharp blow to Sir Ralf Wilcot's strategy and that he advanced in the right direction. He knew that Alfred Hayen could have had various reasons for having committed the murder; and he also knew that he was a greedy and unscrupulous man, but in fact he never prepared any food at the guest house, and the death of Mrs. Luisa Hayen and her daughter Annie was apparently caused by an convoluted collective poisoning plan whose climax was the dinner Mrs. Mary Gautal prepared for the night of 11th of December. Mr. Ernest Lesser also knew that if it wasn't possible to prove fully and clearly the inappropriate relationship between the defendants, which would establish an apparent motive for their actions, Mrs. Mary Gautal would have no motive whatsoever to collaborate or to commit the crime. Therefore, she could not be accused of it.

"Well, you see;" Inspector Fort replied slowly, "physical proof of this intimate relationship doesn't exist, because there's no need for any formalities that may result in a proof. Quite the opposite," mild murmurs and laughter was heard in the hall. "We only rely on the statements of the Donalt family, who although are not claiming to have witnessed something specific, also argue that the relationship between the defendants was not a typical one of a tenant with his landlady. But with all due respect Mr. Lesser, I must remind you that Mrs. Mary Gautal is not in this trial for lewd conduct or immorality, but for having cooked food that resulted as an instrument for this murder."

"Excuse me inspector," interrupted Mr. Ernest Lesser, "I'd like to clarify that according to your report of the investigation, the poison was found in the orange juice, not in the food. Is that correct?"

"For the purposes of this case, it doesn't make any difference," said Inspector Fort. "Remember that the orange juice also came out of Mrs. Mary Gautal's kitchen."

"I have no further questions Judge," said Mr. Ernest Lesser as he returned to his chair.

CHAPTER IX

Mr. Reynold Rell, the court clerk took the oath from Anthony Flynn, the young police officer who was the first person at 113 Lombard Street, after the event occurred. While under oath, he had no doubt that his more than twenty years of experience as a police officer assured him that he was in the middle of a case that would leave its mark on the history of British jurisprudence.

The officer, after his oath, sat down and waited for the interrogation. Sir Ralf Wilcot walked towards him with confident steps, greeted him politely and immediately asked the first question:

"Officer Flyn, can you tell us how you came to find out about this case?"

PC Anthony Flyn licked his lips, rolled his eyes several times, as if seeking the proper order of facts, and finally said:

"You see, prosecutor. I was patrolling my area, when I saw someone running towards me seeking help and I shouted: Here; and went to meet him. As I approached, the man asked me, without offering any explanations, to find a vehicle to transport two sick people to the hospital. He gave me the address where I should go and without waiting for an answer stumbled towards the direction he had come from."

"Agent Flyn, did you see this man afterwards?"

"I did. After arriving at the house located at 113 Lombard Street, I saw him writhing on the floor along with five other people," agent Anthony Flynn said.

"Agent Flyn, could you tell me if it was this man who asked you for help that night?" asked Sir Alfred Wilcot pointing towards Alfred Hayen.

"No, that man was not the man who asked me for help," replied Officer Anthony Flyn, looking intently at Alfred Hayen.

"No more questions, Your Honor," said Sir Ralf Wilcot as he returned to his seat.

Judge David Rogell settled into his chair, ruffled the papers in front of him and turning to the defense attorney Mr. Ernest Lesser, he said:

"Dr. Lesser, do you have any questions for this witness?"

The defense attorney finished making some notes in his notebook, and then answered the magistrate:

"No. I don't think that this witness has anything relevant for solving this case."

CHAPTER X

Dr. Roulf Wensin was expecting Sir Ralf Wilcot's first question. He was self conscious at being the focus of attention.

He remembered, moments ago when he was taking his oath before the court clerk, his voice was barely audible and his legs were shaking. Sweat beaded on his forehead as the voice of the prosecutor reached his ears:

"Tell us, Dr. Wensin, how did you reach the conclusion that the people admitted that night, from 113 Lombard Street to the hospital ward under your direction, were under the effects of a toxin?"

"Their symptoms and my experience as a doctor made it clear."

"Was it then that you communicated your suspicions to the hospital director?"

"In fact, it happened just so," responded Dr. Wensin, now more confidently.

"What did you and Dr. Rust decide then?"

"We ordered blood tests for the patients looking for a toxin and for arsenic in particular, which seemed to be the most likely."

"Dr. Wensin. Does is this type of analysis often performed in the laboratories of civilian hospitals?"

"No, Prosecutor. This type of analysis is performed very rarely in our lab. Forensic medicine laboratories usually make these tests, but we decided to entrust this mission to our own laboratory. We knew our laboratory had the capacity for these purposes and thus we could quickly access and confirm a more accurate diagnosis for our patients."

"Dr. Wensin. What was the result of the analysis?"

"These tests showed that the patients had alarming quantities of arsenic in them Prosecutor."

"Dr. Wensin. I have previous information that the patients underwent another analysis related to the above. Could you elaborate on that?"

"With pleasure, Mr. Prosecutor, I'll tell you. After receiving the results of the first analysis and checking that my suspicions were true, Dr. Rust ordered a second investigation aimed at obtaining the most accurate estimate of the amount of poison in the blood of each patient."

"Dr. Wensin. If you please, inform the court what were the results of the second investigation."

"Strangely, Mr. Prosecutor, those patients with

the largest amount of arsenic in their blood were in better physical condition."

"Could you explain this contradiction, Dr. Wensin?" asked Sir Ralf Wilcot, prompting the doctor to expose his theory on the case.

"Of course I can. After studying the results of the autopsies, having analyzed the work performed in the laboratories, both legal and clinical, and consulting with specialists in toxicology, Dr. Rust and I have come to the conclusion that in this case there was someone who was systematically preparing the bodies of the four survivors with an appropriate dose of arsenic. This procures to create an organic tolerance to the toxic, so that by ingesting a lethal dose they would only suffer a series of minor illnesses and therefore this collective poisoning would appear as a common illness which would rule out any possible suspicion of murder."

"Dr. Wensin, do you have any toxicology knowledge?"

"I do. Toxicology was one of the optional subjects I studied after my graduation."

"Dr. Wensin, do you think it possible that a doctor who would not have any knowledge of toxicology could have detected that the residents of 113 Lombard Street were not suffering a common illness?"

"Initially it would be impossible since it's quite common to see entire families coming to the hospital showing the same symptoms of an illness caused by food poisoning. The difference between this disease and arsenic poisoning, in relation to the clinical symptoms presented by the patient, is minimal; but after twenty four hours from ingesting the poison, marked differences occur. In this particular case, as a result of the preparation to which four of the patients were subjected to in advance, only an error in the amount of arsenic supplied on that night, perhaps fearing that prudential dose would not be effective has enabled me to understand, almost immediately, the reality of the case."

"Dr. Wensin, do you think any of the survivors were in danger of death during the period of hospitalization?"

"Yes. Mrs. Donalt was, among all, in the worst condition. There were times when I thought we would loose her and even now, that we consider her recovered, she still suffers from a slight jaundice and was unable to regain her original weight. We believe that it's a direct result of the amount of toxin that accumulated in her body."

"Dr. Wensin, based on your statements, if the murderer would not have committed an error, as to the amount of arsenic provided that night, and given the preparation of four out of the six people in Mrs. Mary Gautal's guest house, can we conclude that everything would have easily passed as a serious case of gastroenteritis that affected everyone and caused, unfortunately, the death of two inhabitants?"

"We can indeed draw that conclusion."

"One last question, Dr. Wensin: If the deaths of Luisa Hayen and her daughter would have occurred as a result of a common illness, would it have been possible for Mr. Alfred Hayen to refuse to authorize an autopsy on their bodies, given that he was their next of kin?"

"Yes, legally he would have been able to refuse to authorize such autopsy," replied Dr. Wensin.

The defense attorney, Mr. Ernest Lesser, jumped from his seat and angrily objected to Sir Ralf Wilcot's insinuations and Dr. Roulf Wensin statements of an untested theory which had as its sole objective, to confuse the jury.

Judge David Rogell adjusted his glasses with his index finger and said in an almost fatherly tone:

"Mr. Lesser, your objection is overruled."

Dr. Roulf Wensin felt nervous again. He knew that the defense attorney would try to make the most out of the interrogation he was about to make. He felt even more nervous when Mr. Ernest Lesser looked at him questioningly and pointing at him with his index finger, asked:

"Dr. Wensin, how long did it take to get the results of the first analysis?"

"Forty minutes at most, Dr. Lesser."

"Then we can consider that the patients didn't receive adequate medical care, for instance, during the first hour of hospitalization."

"It didn't happen exactly as you put it, Dr. Lesser. Although we had to wait for the results of laboratory reports to confirm our suspicions and be able act in accordance with the diagnosis. I would also like to add that the girl and her mother didn't have, at any time, a real chance to overcome the poisoning and survive."

"No more questions, Your Honor," the defense lawyer abruptly said, in order to interrupt the doctor's speech.

CHAPTER XI

Dr. Boris Hull felt important because it was the first time he had been called to testify before a court, despite the many years he had worked in the hospital laboratory.

Sir Ralf Wilcot walked toward him with measured steps. He stopped at the railing, removed his reading glasses and asked the first question:

"Dr. Hull, could you tell us what were you and your assistant doing at the exact moment when you were entrusted with the task of seeking a toxic in the blood samples of the people who were pointed out in this court by Dr. Rust?"

"We were sterilizing test tubes and beakers."

"You'd be wondering about the reasons for this question, Dr. Hull. I've asked it just to point out that you were well awake so late at night. This shows that you were in a good physical and mental condition for the purposes of this investigation. Am I right or not, Dr. Hull?"

"Yes, you're right."

Dr. Ernest Lesser shifted in his chair; he wished to be able to make an objection, but he realized that nothing would motivate it. He knew that this simple ploy would be another step in favor of Sir Ralf Wilcot. At first glance the observation was insubstantial, but in fact, it ruined his plans in questioning that witness.

"Dr. Hull, said Sir Ralf Wilcot, interrupting thereby the agitated thoughts of Dr. Ernest Lesser, "could you tell us, in the most accurate way possible, the result of that first analysis that the six patients mentioned above underwent."

"Of course, anticipating that you or the defense attorney could ask me that question, I copied the result of the analysis, which I'll read aloud."

Everyone listened attentively as Dr. Boris Hull read the report. As he advanced in his presentation, the faces of everyone present were becoming dismal, unlike the prosecutor's face whose eyes sparkled and whose lips toyed with a triumphant smile. Dr. Ernest Lesser noticed this and his anger reached its climax. He barely managed to control his temper, as he realized that he was still waiting for his turn to question the witness. Dr. Boris Hull finished reading, so Sir Ralf Wilcot asked a new question:

"Thank you, Dr. Hull, for having read the report; but I would also be grateful to know what were the results of the other investigation performed with patients, and the obtained results."

"The Second investigation was also ordered by Dr. Rust, and was aimed at defining the estimated arsenic content in the blood of each patient," said Dr. Boris Hull, adding after a brief pause: "Regarding the investigation results, I informed that these were astounding since those who carried most toxin in their bodies were the patients who were in better physical condition."

"Thank you, Dr. Hull," said Sir Ralf Wilcot, then turning to the judge said: "I have concluded with the witness, Your Honor."

Judge Dr. David Rogell immediately offered the defense attorney the opportunity to question the witness.

Dr. Ernest Lesser advanced decidedly towards the doctor. He saluted and without further ado asked:

"Dr. Hull, how many times did you make this individual estimate for each patient?"

"Only once," answered Dr. Boris Hull.

"Dr. Hull, was it immediately after you obtained blood samples from patients, that they underwent intensive treatment to remove the poison from their bodies?"

"Indeed," said Dr. Boris Hull.

"Dr. Hull, what can you tell us about the probability that the recipients containing the patients' blood samples may have been mixed up therefore leading to such astounding results?" asked Dr. Ernest Lesser emphatically.

"Objection, Your Honor!" said Sir Ralf Wilcot. "This is an insult to the medical profession and an offense to the British Crown. The insinuations proffered by the defense attorney are simply unacceptable."

"Objection sustained," stressed Judge Dr. David Rogell, to add then as a recrimination: "Dr. Lesser, stick to the facts or theories that have solid foundations or are based on concrete evidence. Don't try to put into question the morale and prestige of men who deserve our admiration and respect, from a selfless and humane profession."

Sir Ralf Wilcot sat and smiled slightly. The jury was humbled by the judge's words. The silence was total, when the judge's voice was heard again:

"Dr. Lesser, you may continue'"

"That's all, Your Honor. I have concluded with this witness," said the defense attorney as he retreated to his seat.

"In this case, I end the session for today. We'll continue tomorrow at 10:00 a.m."

CHAPTER XII

The press severely criticized the attitude assumed by the defense attorney Dr. Ernest Lesser. In the journalists' opinion, this approach reflected the defense lawyer's inability to defend himself against the attacks of the prosecutor, Sir. Ralph Wilcot, who, as a skilled professional accustomed to success, had already managed to gain an advantage over his opponent, the young and inexperienced lawyer. Wilcot's first achievement, in the opinion of the journalists, was the brilliant idea he had of calling Inspector Joe Fort from Scotland Yard as a witness, to indirectly formulate the charges against the accused. The second one is attributed to the moment when the prosecutor asked Officer Anthony Flynn, if the defendant was the person who had asked for help that night, so as to make it precisely clear who stayed in the house that night, Mrs. Mary Gautal, Mrs. Jeannie Donalt and Mr. Alfred Hayen as well as Mrs. Luisa Hayen and little Annie Bannet, who were unconscious.

As for the benefits Dr. Roulf Wensin and Dr. Boris Hull' interventions as witnesses brought to the case of the prosecution, reporters assured the public that it was unnecessary to comment upon, given the disagreement between the defense attorney and the judge.

It was 10 a.m. when the hearing resumed. As soon as he was granted permission to speak, Sir Ralf Wilcot didn't hesitate to request a public reading of the autopsies report on the bodies of Mrs. Luisa Hayen and her daughter Annie, stating that for him, this exceptional report was pertinent to the case. The court clerk Mr. Reynold Rell began to read aloud:

"Outline of the forensic report resulting from the autopsies on the bodies of Mrs. Luisa Hayen and the young Annie Bannet, and I quote," the secretary paused for a moment and then continued, "Forensic examinations carried out on the bodies of Mrs. Luisa Hayen and her daughter Annie Bannet, show the following results: the cause of death occurred as a direct result of respiratory paralysis, caused by poisoning due to ingestion of arsenic anhydride, which led, subsequently to heart failure. Other complementary insights that helped in verifying the ingestion of arsenic anhydride, observed in the cadavers are:

a) Inflammation of the gastro-intestinal glands.

b) Fatty degeneration of the liver, heart and vascular linings.

That's all, Your Honor," said the court secretary after reading the document.

"Thank you," replied the magistrate, who then added addressing Sir Ralf Wilcot: "The prosecution may continue."

"Thank you, Your Honor. That's all I needed to hear in reference to the forensic examination. The truth is that I wish that the coroners in charge of the autopsy, had included more in their report as to the amount of arsenic found in the corpses; but I think that having heard the report, it's not necessary to request a new forensic examination. Of course, if the defense attorney doesn't decide otherwise," he said turning to Dr. Ernest Lesser, who churned uneasily in his seat.

"The defense attorney may speak now," said the judge.

"I don't consider my speech necessary at this time Your Honor," bellowed the defense attorney.

CHAPTER XIII

A murmur swept the room when the next witness, Dr. Richard Brook from the laboratories of Scotland Yard, was announced.

Dr. Brook moved slowly down the aisle. He crossed the space left free by the short railings held open by the court clerk, who with Bible in hand was ready to take the oath. The doctor stopped in front of the witness chair facing the room. He waited for the arrival of the secretary. He placed his right hand on the thick book and repeated the oath mechanically. He then glanced around to the jury and carefully observed the judge and then the accused. Then he looked at the defense attorney and found him to be slightly uneasy. He shifted his sight again to see the graceful figure of the prosecutor, Sir Ralph Wilcot, who looked as if he were thoroughly studying him, then said:

"Dr. Brook, in abusing your generosity, I'd like to expose to the jury some elements that will make a different in this case, where medical science has been the determining factor throughout the period of investigation," the prosecutor said as he walked towards the table by the judge's chair. Once there, he continued:

"Ladies and gentlemen of the jury, before I start to question Dr. Brook, I would like to point out something for you. In all cases processed in this room, this table is intended to serve as a seat for anything that might constitute evidence for investigation; however, this time it's empty! The more observant of you may have wondered why this is so. Some may have come to think that evidence is lacking. Others might still be waiting for the moment when evidence is revealed to know its true extent. For everyone, wherever you stand, I have to inform you that this time the evidence is far from here, in the building of the Laboratory of Forensic Medicine in London; but here we can rely on the reports that tell us exactly what's there," he said pointing to a small pile of papers that were stacked on the corner of the table, and continued: "If I previously omitted to point out this detail, it was with the deliberate intention of seeking the right opportunity, and this seems to be the time. So I ask you to listen carefully to every word that this witness has to say."

That said, he stood in front of Dr. Richard Brook, he put on his spectacles, and began to read to himself the notes he had written in a small notebook, which he had just taken from the inside pocket of his jacket. When he finished reading, he approached the witness and said:

"Dr. Brook, I beg you to let everyone present know the results of the investigation you undertook starting with the examination of the elements collected in the presence of Inspector Joe Fort, at the crime scene."

Dr. Richard Brook appeared to remain absent minded for a moment, then said with a calm voice:

"I could start with tea residues; then the sugar cubes I picked up in the kitchen and then the piece of fabric that was part of a tablecloth, which had fresh samples of a drink; although it would be best to start with our arrival at 113Lombard Street and my first impressions. Yes, that'll do," the witness said to him before continuing. "When Inspector Fort and I entered the hall of the house, he noticed the large stain that was in the middle of the room. We approached carefully, so as not to spoil any evidence that might be used as samples. We had no doubt the stain was vomit, distinguished by the stench and the characteristic pungent odor particular to human vomit; secondly, because we could observe evidence of half chewed food which allowed us to see clearly its origin and nature. We took samples for later analysis. Next, we went to the dining room where we didn't find any clues of great interest since the floor looked well swept and everything was in order and tidied up. From the dining room, we went to the kitchen, where we could only find leftovers of tea, since the other dishes used during dinner had been already washed and put away. There, the inspector insisted that we take samples of the sugar, in case it contained anything that might provide us with the slightest clue. We were about to finish and leave when the inspector noticed a white tablecloth with spots on one of its edges. I proceeded to cut a piece of the stained tablecloth with a pair of scissors, isolated the sample and placed it properly with the other collected samples. Then we toured the house again looking for anything that might look suspicious, but this was in vain. That was my first visit to the crime scene and, therefore, my first contact with the elements related to this case."

Dr. Richard Brook paused to take a sip of water. Once he put the glass back into place, he set out to bluntly answer the question the prosecutor asked:

"Well, we found no abnormalities in the tea or in the sugar, Prosecutor, but when analyzing samples of vomit I encountered the presence of arsenic oxide or something very similar to this. As for the tablecloth piece, it had several stains that were undoubtedly orange juice; on both the center and the edge of this, we could see a substance which matched the one previously found in the vomit, or one of the derivatives of arsenic, presumably arsenic oxide or anhydride. The part of the tablecloth that was stain free showed no signs of any of those substances. This demonstrates that the toxin was not present on the fabric of the tablecloth, neither on the floor of the house, since we also took and analyzed samples from places in the room that were not contaminated with vomit. Thus, I can conclude that the poison was contained in food ingested by the victims. In addition, I believe that all the arsenic derivatives, ingested by the inhabitants of 113 Lombard Street that night, was in the orange juice."

"Dr. Brook," interrupted the prosecutor, "did you rely during the investigative process on any assistants who can testify about your work methods and your handling of the material evidence, should we need to verify your efficient findings?"

"Of course, Prosecutor, Dr. Laranlencie and my assistant, laboratory technician Gustav Rich, both worked with me. They also participated in the second investigation that I conducted in this case," said Dr. Richard Brook.

"I'll ask the secretary of this court to please take note of the names of the people Dr. Brook just mentioned."

"Yes, Your Honor," came the secretary's response.

"You may continue with the presentation, Dr. Brook," said Dr. Rogell to the witness.

"Thank you, Your Honor. The second time Inspector Fort and I met for the purposes of this investigation, was when he came to pick me up to go to the crime scene in order to look for any containers that might reveal the rat poison. Once there and after a thorough investigation, we found three small metal containers with some whitish paste which seemed to be what we were looking for. Then we decided to conduct a new house search, believing that it might reveal something of interest that might have been missed, on our first visit. After an hour of searching, Inspector Fort called me loudly. His excitement was due to the fact that the compact powder box on Mrs. Mary Gautal's bedroom dressing table contained a whitish ash. I simply collected the ashes without expecting to find anything relevant there, but once I arrived at the lab I set to work immediately on the newly collected samples. We first analyzed the alleged rat poison paste and we were surprised to find that it was actually common talc, instead of arsenic; but we were even more astonished when we got the results of analyzing the ash Inspector Fort found in the compact box. That ash corresponded to burned paper and a product that we was not similar to any of those used in the manufacture of cosmetics. Therefore we subjected the ashes to a special procedure and after much effort we determined that it was a derivative of arsenic. Apparently whoever burned the envelope containing the product thought that in doing so, they would eliminate any possible trace. This is all I have to say."

"Thanks for your report, Dr. Brook," said the prosecutor, and continued as he walked to his chair: "Your Honor. I have finished with the witness."

"The witness is available for the defense attorney. It's your turn Mr. Lesser," said the judge.

Dr. Ernest Lesser was deep in thought. 'What to say? What to do against all that body of evidence? How to get any advantage from the statements of the man who knew his facts so confidently? How to get out of that difficult situation now that everyone looked at him expectantly for his next words? How…'

"Dr. Lesser. The witness is yours," repeated Judge David Rogell.

Dr. Ernest Lesser stood. The judge's voice, summoning him back to reality meant that he had to get out of his inertia. He looked intently at Dr. Richard Brook, and addressing the highest authority in the room shouted:

"The Defense has no questions for this witness."

CHAPTER XIV

      Dr. Carl Pamer was shaking. While it's true that it was a bit cold, the fact that his shivering was somewhat exaggerated remained. Even his voice shook as he took the oath. Most shaky of all was when he directed a sidelong glance toward the stand where the jury was immersed in deathly silence. He could see that all eyes were fixed on him. Suddenly, he noticed that the prosecutor had gotten up from his seat and was heading toward him. He feared and rightly so because he had heard Sir Ralf Wilcot sometimes used to depart from the case discussed in court, to virtually suggest investigations of the witnesses, if he suspected that these were hiding any valuable information or their activities were not entirely legal. But he expected no problems, planning to say everything he knew and escape this mess as soon as possible.

      The prosecutor stood before him and greeted him. Then he looked at him as if he were a stuffed animal on display in taxidermy shop, and without further ado, he asked:

"Dr. Carl Pamer, do you recognize the accused?"

Dr. Carl Pamer stared at both of them.

"Yes. I have seen him before," he said and immediately thought: 'How could I forget someone who had asked me for a prescription for arsenic, to prepare a rat poison when there are such good products for this purpose available on the market? How could I have thought at the time that they were a couple of maniacs that would bring me nothing but trouble? I thought them to be cheap and greedy people; but not for a moment I could imagine ...'

Suddenly, the prosecutor's voice interrupted his thoughts:

"Dr. Carl Pamer, did you hear my question?"

"Oh yes." He replied mechanically.

"Well, you may start by answering when you're ready," invited the prosecutor.

"You see... I saw the gentleman for the first time in my office, when he came to ask for a prescription for some derivative of arsenic, as he wanted to prepare a paste in order to exterminate a plague of mice that had invaded the house where he lived."

"Allow me to interrupt you, Dr. Pamer, but I wonder if it's customary in your office to issue such prescriptions," asked the prosecutor.

"No. I have never before given someone a prescription of this kind," replied Dr Pamer.

"Are you sure of that, Dr. Pamer?" the prosecutor asked.

"Yes, I'm sure," replied the doctor.

"How can you explain then that three pharmacies in your area have reported recently selling this product, using prescriptions covered by your signature?" The prosecutor asked ironically.

Dr. Carl Pamer froze. His worst fear materialized. Sir Ralf Wilcot had derailed slightly from the case in question and started soiling his integrity and embarrassing him. His own thoughts confused him and since he could not find an immediate exit, he decided to play the prosecutor:

"You see... I'm a little nervous because I have never confronted this situation before ... And now I come to think that it seems to me that you have some reason for asking this. Now I remember that I had in fact issued similar prescriptions to some friends who were confronted with the same mice problem. Of course, I was very careful to explain to them how dangerous the product can be and how it must be used in accordance to the particular needs of each household and I only issued prescriptions for the amount required to be used on each occasion," said the doctor.

"Tell me, Dr. Pamer. Did you explain all this to the defendants?"

"I tried to but he insisted he knew how to use it and in which proportions."

"Didn't you find such knowledge suspicious Dr. Pamer?"

"Well ... I thought... I only ..." Dr. Carl Pamer stammered awkwardly while wiping a bead of sweat on his forehead with his handkerchief.

"I see you are getting yourself all warmed up, Dr. Pamer; you're no longer shaking as before."

"Yes!" The doctor smiled nervously.

"Tell me, Dr. Pamer. When and where did you first see that lady?"

Dr. Carl Pamer looked at the defendants wanting to annihilate them.

"I've seen her in my office just a few days after the visit of the gentleman."

"What brought the defendant into your office, Dr. Pamer?"

"She wanted a prescription to buy arsenic," said the doctor as he showed even more intense sweating.

"Tell me, Dr. Pamer. What was your reaction this time?"

"Well ... this ... I'll tell you ... you see ..."

"Stop trying to find a way out of this, doctor! You certainly issued the prescription! How could you refuse when that meant good money for your pocket?" sentenced the prosecutor.

Dr. Carl Pamer could not cope anymore. He had just reached the end of his tether. He felt cornered, in despair. He loosened his tie in a vain attempt to allow a breath of fresh air and ease his convulsions. He felt suffocated, unable to breathe, so addressing the judge, he said:

"Your Honor, I can't take it anymore. I can't cope. This man stuns me, I'm in despair, I can't breathe. Your Honor, in other words, I refuse to continue answering the prosecutor's interrogation."

"Unfortunately, Dr. Pamer, the prosecutor is entitled to continue asking questions and so far he has not committed any offense worthy of reproach," was the reply of Dr. Rogell.

Dr. Carl Pamer slumped down in his chair. He covered his face with both his hands and hid there for several seconds. Then he raised his head as he dropped his arms in defeat. When his gaze stumbled upon the prosecutor, who say simply:

"Continue."

"Thank you, Dr. Pamer. I have finished with the witness, Your Honor," said the prosecutor on his way to his seat.

The judge had authorized the defense attorney's witness interrogation more than a minute ago. Dr. Carl Pamer, meanwhile, looked a little calmer. Even the handkerchief constantly in use during Sir Ralf Wilcot's questions, rested untouched in the pocket of his jacket.

Dr. Ernest Lesser stood. He carefully looked at the face of each of the members of the jury. He glanced at the reporters. He stared at the defendants, seeking a guiding gesture that may serve for getting something favorable out of that witness; but there was no answer, no clue, no hints, so addressing the judge, said:

"The defense does not consider it necessary to take a statement from this witness."

CHAPTER XV

Dr. Ernest Lesser was tidying up the documentation on his desk, feigning a serenity that he didn't feel lately. Only the Donalts' testimonies were missing and he knew that their statements would be decisive for the outcome of the case. Both witnesses could help change the impression that the court had on the defendants or on the contrary could further accentuate the perception that they were guilty. The outcome of the court case was soon coming as an avalanche. Donalt Jeannie walked down the aisle towards the witness stand.

"Mrs. Jeannie Donalt, repeat after me!"

Rell Reynold's voice dominated the room as he read the oath.

Once the witness accepted her responsibilities to society, the judge ordered the prosecutor to proceed in taking the witness's statement. Sir Ralf Wilcot went towards her in his usual steady pace. Mrs. Jeannie Donalt seemed hypnotized. While keeping her gaze on the accused, a sickly pallor suddenly gripped her. Her mouth, with thin but shapely lips, straightened and contracted in an atrocious grimace. Sir Ralf Wilcot realized that the witness was not in a position to give evidence and needed his help, which is why he asked:

"Mrs. Donalt. Are you ill? Can I help you with anything?"

His questions were lost in a void. The silence that followed was profound, dumbfounding. The prosecutor repeated the same questions, but received no response from the witness. When he asked the judge whether he thought the presence of a doctor was necessary to attend to the Canadian, Mrs. Jeannie Donalt stood. For a moment the prosecutor had the impression that the witness had decided not to testify; but his suspicion was brief. Mrs. Jeannie Donalt pointed with a blaming gesture toward the spot where the defendants sat. The woman's body began to shake. Her eyes seemed to be ready to pop out of their sockets. Her mouth began to lose rigidity. She took a deep breath and leaving her place started moving toward the defendants shouting loudly: "Murderers! Murderers!" The prosecutor tried to cut her off; but it was impossible. The court clerk and the bailiff of the room hurriedly stood in the witness's way managing to prevent her reaching the place were the defendants sat. The court continued to hear her shouts: "Murderers!" "Child murderers!" "Criminals!" "Damn you!" Mrs. Mary Gautal could no longer control her nerves and began to cry, in a hysterical fit. The witness was virtually dragged out of the room, while continuing to curse and insult the defendants. Great confusion dominated the atmosphere. Sir Ralf Wilcot came back to his seat to make it easier for the judge to try and restore the order in the room, when he heard a murmur that was growing with every second. He raised his head instinctively to seek the source of that new unrest and his gaze lingered on the figure of Mrs. Mary Gautal. She cried, leaning over Alfred Hayen's shoulder with her hands around his neck. The prosecutor stood and without asking permission to speak, began to shout:

"Look at them! Look everyone! See for yourselves what we needed to prove! Decide for yourselves!"

Dr. Ernest Lesser joined in with a brandishing objection:

"I object Your Honor! Objection! The prosecutor is trying to take advantage of a completely logical reaction among two human beings who are subjected to a stressful situation!"

Dr. David Rogell repeatedly banged his gavel while calling for order. Tempers calmed down almost completely, opportunity the judge took to say:

"Today's session is adjourned. We shall continue tomorrow at 9:30 am."

CHAPTER XVI

It was about eleven at night and Mary Gautal was alone in her cell. She was no longer crying. She had come to the conclusion that everyone believed her guilty and therefore she will be sent to the gallows; but she didn't plan to offer the spectacle of a public execution. Whatever Alfred Hayen did, ceased to concern her, but as far as she was concerned, she had already made a decision. She called the guard who was reading in the light in front of her cell. He rose slowly and went wearily to attend to the prisoner. When he was in front of her, he asked:

"What do you want?"

"A cup of tea, please. I have a terrible headache."

"I'll go get it for you. It will take only a few minutes."

"One more favor, guard. Could you turn off the lamp for a little while? The light disturbs me and I can't sleep."

"I'm afraid I can't do that right now but I will when I get back. Of course, I'll have to turn it on again once you have fallen asleep."

"Thank you so much. You can't imagine how much I appreciate it."

"It's my pleasure to serve others. I'll be back in a few minutes with your cup of tea."

Mrs. Mary Gautal waited for him, leaning against the bars of her cell. She took the metal cup in which the guard had brought her tea in her hands without changing her position and took a long sip of the dark liquid. She stood observing the guard in the light of the incandescent bulb in front of her cell as he walked to his chair at the end of the hallway to continue reading. When she was fully convinced that she was no longer within the visual sight of her guard, she rushed to her bed and pulled out from under the mattress three long strips that she had ripped from her jacket during the time the jailer had gone to get the tea. She tested the strength of each and took to the task of weaving them to give them more resistance. Once the work was finished, she went quietly to the floor of her cell. She made a noose at one end of the braid and tied the other end to the upper link to the chain that held the board that served as a bed, which was about four feet high. Then she knelt on the bed, her back against the wall, stuck her head through the loop, adjusted it to her neck and dropped heavily towards the floor in her prison cell.

CHAPTER XVII

Mr. David Rogel was just concluding his presentation of the new developments concerning the case, when he requested to call Mrs. Jeannie Donalt as a witness.

This time around, the Canadian portrayed an attitude that was clearly different from her previous appearance in court. She was now calm and her gaze was soft and serene. Although most of the time she remained despondent and withdrawn. She noticed the prosecutor's presence in front of her. She squinted, barely raising her head and said softly:

"You may start whenever you deem convenient."

Sir Ralf Wilcot wordlessly observed the witness for a while. He was trying to scrutinize the thoughts that dominated this woman after being informed of Mrs. Mary Gautal's suicide. The woman remained elusive, head down, trying to hide her face and eyes.

"Mrs. Donalt," the prosecutor began saying, "I see no reason why you should feel distressed at hearing about Mrs. Mary Gautal's death. The reasons that led to the defendant's suicide, at no time can be directly related to your recent speech in this room. It was her own conscience that would not allow her to continue living."

"Objection! Your Honor," interrupted Mr. Dr. Ernest Lesser. "The prosecutor speaks of the deceased in such a manner that establishes her indisputable guilt in relation to the facts and this could negatively impact the jury's verdict with regards of my other defendant."

"Objection admitted. I request the prosecutor to limit himself to comment on proven facts and elements with solid foundations not aimed at confusing the jury," said the judge.

"Excuse me, Your Honor, it will not happen again."

Silence reigned. The prosecutor turned to face the witness, and said:

"Mrs. Donalt, would you kindly inform us of facts you may consider relevant to solving this case?"

Mrs. Jeannie Donalt began her story. The jury was absorbed in her statement. Every gesture of her face was observed, every word out of her mouth was listened to intently. Brief periods of silence occurred, when she referred to little Annie. However, her boldness was manifest when reporting any events regarding the defendants. She was even tougher when referring to the time she was hospitalized and the emotional consequences affecting her after the facts. Suddenly she stopped and plunged into a deep silence. The prosecutor became aware of his witness emotional unrest and not wanting to lose the magic of the moment, he immediately asked.

"Mrs. Donalt. According to your opinion, what was the type of relations the defendants had with each other?"

The witness reacted, shocked by the question. She straightened to her full height and stated:

"Recent events speak for themselves, Mr. Prosecutor."

"Thank you, Mrs. Donalt," the prosecutor said to the witness and, turning to the judge, he added: "I have concluded with this witness, Your Honor."

"The defense may proceed in taking the witness's statements," said Judge David Rogell.

Dr. Ernest Lesser directed his steps towards the witness, stood before her and looked directly at the jury. When he was sure he had everyone's attention, he asked:

"Mrs. Donalt before Mrs. Mary Gautal's nervous shock a few days ago that perhaps could have induced the court to a misconception of the relations that existed between her and Mr. Alfred Hayen, did you have a chance to listen, observe or notice any concrete facts that could serve as a basis for the assumption that the two maintained an intimate relationship?"

The room fell silent. The witness was deep in thought and quiet for a long time. Suddenly, defense counsel's voice was heard again, repeating the question. Mrs. Jeannie Donalt reacted and finally said.

"Concrete facts, no, but ..."

"We can establish then that, it was the first time you saw Mrs. Mary Gautal embrace my client."

"Yes sir."

"Mrs. Donalt. How was your relationship with your landlady'"

"It was very good."

"Was there ever any animosity between you two?"

"No."

"Mrs. Donalt. Do you consider my client a daring man?"

"So I've heard."

"Mrs. Donalt. Has my client ever made you feel uncomfortable in any way?"

Mrs. Jeannie Donalt flushed. She understood the defense attorney's insinuation and where he wanted to lead her with his insinuations. She confronted him with a look that reflected her anger and told him:

"You must know Sir, that I am very happy with my husband. I've never felt any affinity towards your disgusting client and if I am here it's only because I believe that the murder of an innocent child can't go unpunished."

A murmur dominated the room. The defense attorney stepped to the podium and pointing to the accused asked the witness:

"Mrs. Donalt. Assuming that my client was sentenced to death, would you be able to act as the executioner and execute the verdict?"

"If necessary I would," replied the Canadian.

"For my part, I have concluded, Judge. This lady's animosity toward my client hinders the emergence of the truth and endangers the clarity of this process, therefore, as a defense attorney, I ask for the testimony of this witness to be dismissed."

CHAPTER XVIII

Mr. Paul Donalt was the last witness on the list. Sir Ralf Wilcot had his plan well laid out. He would allow the Canadian to make a comprehensive statement of the facts and then ask him some specific questions in order to get answers aimed at directly influencing the jury's perceptions. The prosecutor approached the witnesses stand, greeted the Canadian and without further ado, said:

"Mr. Donalt, could you please share with us all the facts or data that you're aware of and feel it may be relevant to solving this murder?"

Paul Donalt's statement was extensive and explicit. He started with making a long and detailed exposition of daily life in the guest house and only stopped when he referred to the time when Mrs. Mary Gautal prompted him to go in search for help after the events on the night of 11th of December. The prosecutor understood the importance of asking a question at this exact moment, and resting his right hand on the railing of the short witness stand, he addressed the Canadian:

"Mr. Donalt, have you considered, at any point that there may have been an ulterior motive for being asked to go and search for help?"

"After I found out about the cause of death of Annie and Mrs. Luisa, I thought that maybe I was sent in search of help so I could be out of the way and not prevent the destruction of any evidence."

Silence reigned in the room. The witness had fallen silent and slouched into a defensive position. He seemed shocked and deeply affected by recalling of the facts. Suddenly he straightened to continue saying:

"The only detail I have left to add is that, when I returned to the guest house, I found everyone lying on the floor, vomiting and suffering from terrible convulsions."

The witness fell silent again. He sank his face into his hands and remained silent. A murmur spread through the room.

"Mr. Donalt. I must ask you to make an effort and control your emotions. Individual expressions of feelings can affect the jury's perception of the actual facts," asked Dr. David Rogell, in a compassionate but severe tone. Then adding after a short pause: "I ask the jury to dismiss any perception that they may have received due to the witness's emotional expressions during his testimony and to adhere only to the facts."

Sir Ralf Wilcot realized that the jury was affected psychologically, so he addressed a new question to the witness.

"Mr. Donalt. Have you ever wondered what could have been the motive of this heinous murder?"

"What was the motive?" asked the witness.

"Yes!"

"Selfishness and betrayal!" replied the witness.

"Could you be more specific, please?" said Sir Ralf Wilcot.

"Well, I'll try to please you. Mrs. Mary Gautal was selfish for having an intimate relationship with a man who was married to someone else. Betrayal corresponds to Mr. Alfred Hayen. First he betrayed the trust put in him by Luisa, when she handed him the administration of all her estate, a small fortune that he squandered without any consideration. Secondly, he betrayed his wife again in order to find an ally to help him carry out his murderous plans," responded the witness.

"Mr. Donalt, could you explain how come you believe that there were two people involved in the murder?" the prosecutor asked.

"Objection, Your Honor! I object!" Mr. Ernest Lesser shouted angrily as he rose from his seat defiantly. "The prosecutor once again is fishing for assumptions and personal assessments intended only to confuse the jurors."

"Objection denied, Dr. Lesser! While the prosecution departs from the facts, I believe that he does so seeking to clarify concepts and to obtain firsthand information from an exceptional witness residing with the victims and the defendants," Judge Dr. David Rogell stated.

After the judge's speech, an approving hum sounded around the room and it only ceased when the judge called for order inviting Mr. Paul Donalt to answer the question asked by the prosecutor.

"In my opinion Mrs. Mary Gautal was the hand of the murderous plan because she had direct access to the foods all of us consumed. As for Alfred Hayen, I'm sure it was him, the one who devised, organized and directed the entire plan," said the Canadian.

"Mr. Donalt," interrupted the prosecutor, "there's still a question concerning an important part of the crime, and although no one has yet brought this up, I noticed it still causes uncertainty among the jurors and I would like it if it's possible for you to clarify where you believe the defendant was been able to obtain the information that was necessary to carry out a crime as technically complicated and as dangerous as this, even for experts in the medical sciences and pharmaceutical industries."

A murmur of approval went around the room. Dr. Ernest Lesser realized that at that precise moment the fate of his client was decided. 'How come it hadn't occurred to him to ask that question first?' he wondered. 'What game was the prosecutor playing at on this occasion? What was his new strategy? What did the prosecutor knew that he didn't?'

Paul Donalt smiled. He focused his gaze towards the place where the defendant was seated, saying:

"I trust that everyone knows that before Mrs. Mary Gautal occupied the building located on 113 Lombard Street, the place used to be a drugstore. When moving to another location, the drugstore's owners left behind several objects, among which there were some books and manuals.

Among those manuals there was a treaty of pharmacology, which Mrs. Gautal found. However, this treaty became the exclusive property of Mr. Alfred Hayen who so interested in it that no one else got a chance to get their hands on it since he took it upon himself to carry the book to his bedroom every night, instead of leaving it on the coffee table where it belonged and where he also used to sit and read."

"With your permission, Mr. Donalt, interrupted the prosecutor, "do you know whether Mr. Alfred Hayen reread some of the pages of the book in particular?"

"Although I'm rather embarrassed to admit it, I have been ill mannered and I allowed curiosity to get the best of me. I carefully observed him, in order to find out which pages he reread daily, so that, if at any point in the future I got my hands on that treaty, I'd find out which topic had kept Alfred so absorbed in reading. So I can assure you, without harboring any doubt whatsoever that the recurring theme of Alfred Hayen's particular interest in that book, is to be found among pages 235 to 248," said the witness."

When Sir Ralf Wilcot heard the certainty with which the Canadian spoke, he went to his desk, picked up a heavy package containing a voluminous book. He returned to where the witness was seated and showing him the book, asking:

"Mr. Donalt. Is this the book to which you refer?"

"That is indeed the book," affirmed the witness, revealing a great degree of astonishment.

"Are you absolutely sure? Please look at it carefully, Mr. Donalt," asked the prosecutor as he handed the witness the heavy volume, in order to confirm whether it was the same as the Canadian had seen on previous occasions in the guest house.

"I'm absolutely sure. This undoubtedly is the same copy that Mr. Alfred Hayen used to read on a daily basis," the witness answered.

Sir Ralf Wilcot directed himself to the judge and holding out the voluminous book, said:

"I came to know of the existence of this treaty about the use of toxins, on a visit to the crime scene. I took it and brought it to court to present it as an alternative proof. I didn't previously present this as proof because I was waiting for an adequate opportunity and I believe there is no better time than this. In addition, I also took this treaty to the pharmacology and fingerprinting department and allow me to present the report issued by the experts, Your Honor," the prosecutor said as he handed it over in a sealed envelope and then continued:

"The fingerprints that are best detected on the pages of this treaty correspond to the former soldier Alfred Hayen. Many of these fingerprints are to be found on the upper corners of the pages of the book, between pages 235 to 248, so we concluded that these were indeed the pages consulted by Mr. Hayen with more frequency. Please note that the report coincides with the witness' statements. Moreover, I'd like to point out that the topic of the aforementioned pages focuses exclusively on the regulated use of strychnine as an effective drug in the treatment of asthenia and arsenic for other diseases. These pages are also explaining the formulas and the mode of administration of these substances. As far as I am concerned, I consider that I have said everything I had to say; I have finished interrogating this witness, Your Honor."

Dr. Ernest Lesser stood before the witness. He knew that unless a miracle would happen, his client would be convicted. He thought of challenging the presentation of the treaty as evidence by the prosecution; but its validity was overwhelming. He was sure that the case was lost and he also knew that the witness before him vehemently showed his desire to lead his testimony to the execution of the defendant, which is why he planned to limit his questions and seek contradictions in the witness's reply.

"Mr. Donalt," at last the defense lawyer spoke, "could you tell me what is the reason for your manifest hatred towards my client?"

Without stopping to think for a second, the Canadian replied:

"He murdered one of the people that I loved most in my life. Don't you think this is a sufficient reason to hate him?"

"Your Honor, members of the jury," said Dr. Ernest Lesser in a calm tone, "as you must have noticed, the witness is not impartial. Therefore I have no choice but to finish questioning him believing him to be not suitable in the search of justice, given the petty feelings of revenge that this man harbors towards my client."

CHAPTER XIX

"Don't think for a moment that I fear your decision regarding my person," were the first words that sprang from Mr. Alfred Hayen's lips, when the judge authorized his speech, after he refused to testify before the prosecution or the defense.

"Whatever happens, I am willing to accept it with dignity and courage. I know very well that the evidence is overwhelmingly against me, including the fact that the fountain of knowledge, which could have provided anyone with the tools necessary to make such a complicated crime possible, was within my reach. I understand all that, as I also understand that I can't expect you to take a decision in my favor. If to purge a crime I have not committed, I shall be sent to prison; from there I will endeavor to find the real murderer. If on the contrary I shall be sentenced to death, I will try to make the most of every minute of life, knowing that I haven't gotten much time left. Don't think that I am used to living life this way; it's not like this. This way of thinking dates back only a few days ago and has welled up in me and strengthened me as I have had to face this situation of being accused and tried for a crime I didn't commit, while finding it quite impossible to escape and feeling powerless in any attempt to prove my innocence. To make matters worse, the person responsible for representing the public against me is nobody else but Sir Ralf Wilcot, a man who undoubtedly has the skill to make you see red as black. Of course I can't even blame him. Since I know that for him it's more important to win a complicated case in order to further increase his already enormous prestige, than the fate of an innocent being on the face of the earth. However, I don't hold grudges. What I do regret is the fact that I am not able to find the murderer or whoever planned this hoax against me and poor Mary Gautal who had such a heartbreaking end of life. I would have liked to find out who the murderer was and congratulate him for such a thorough, efficient and well-organized plan. It's all I have to say, Your Honor."

CHAPTER XX

Sir Ralf Wilcot had been ordered to present his findings to the court. His slender figure stood out even more due to the precise cut of his dark gray suit. He walked slowly toward the middle of the court. He ran his gaze over all attendees in the room, and walking slowly towards the place where the jury was seated, then started talking in a calm and thoughtful voice:

"Your Honor, Honorable members of the jury, Dr. Ernest Lesser - dear colleague, who so brilliantly led the defense of this case, members of the press, ladies and gentlemen in this room, together we are treading the rough path that must lead us to find justice for this case, for which the investigation featured relevant evidence that emerged through applying scientific, criminology and forensic techniques. The laboratories and chemical specialists have been the real experts on this occasion. This, in itself, has caused me to abandon my customary manner of working in court, forcing me to work more with your reasoning than with the little existing evidence. Of course, in referring to the insufficient evidence, which traditionally, is so important when a case is analyzed. Cases in which I have acted as prosecutor have been plentiful during my career and I have encountered criminals of all kinds, from sadists to the mentally ill. I have come across people who committed criminal acts in moments of utter despair, despite being, upstanding citizens of unimpeachable morality. To better understand some types of criminals, let me review the typical conduct of some of them. Let us begin with the sadist.

It's usually an individual suffering from a disease or an imbalance that urges him to wickedness and depravity. This type of criminal almost always targets his crimes towards the opposite sex, either out of spite or just for pleasure. Usually they are captured quickly and those who manage to evade justice do not get to cause more than seven deaths before being captured. However, there have been criminals with this profile, who have caused greater damages to humanity.

Another specific case is those who suffer from a mental illness that urges them to kill in order to satisfy a criminal instinct. This type of criminal has no distinction of sex and, in most cases, no apparent reason. As for the damage they can cause to humanity, until they are captured, it's similar to the previous typology.

There are murderers who have committed crimes for many motives. However, the type of murderer who in a moment of clouded judgment can't control his impulses and ignoring society and its laws is more abundant. Let me emphasize that this type of murderer repents of his actions in ninety percent of the cases. I want to point out that the act of committing a crime is mostly due to a state of chronic mental disturbance of the criminal. This means that if the ninety percent of the criminals, who are in perfect mental health, would have stopped to think for a few minutes before committing the crime; they would not have carried out the action.

Returning to the case in question, I'd like to inform you that the defendants underwent medical tests to establishing their mental health. These tests showed that both enjoyed excellent mental health and were in command of all their mental faculties. Therefore showing no symptoms whatsoever of psychological trauma, sexual alienation or psychopathic behavior. Similarly, I should also clarify that the suicide of the defendant Mrs. Mary Gautal has been considered by many as her only escape from the punishment of the law. It demonstrates that she must have been sure to be found guilty and without any chance of salvation."

"Objection, Your Honor!" Dr. Ernest Lesser shouted. "The prosecutor is using irrelevant personal assumptions of a few people with the deliberate purpose of influencing the jury's decision and at this time it can't even be argued that the hypothesis has been formulated by science. On the contrary, it's only the journalists' speculations on the truth and the assumptions and deductions of ordinary people influenced by it."

"Objection sustained. The court urges the prosecution to not stray from the facts and evidence proven during this trial," the judge sentenced.

Sir Ralf Wilcot smirked. That warning did nothing more than to focus the jurors' attention on the reasons that led Mrs. Mary Gautal's suicide. He adjusted his tie and restarted his lecture:

"If this had been a crime committed in any other way, it would not have much importance with regard to the safety of our society. Just think of the cold blood a person needs to perform a crime that requires careful execution by following a methodical plan for a period ranging from five to ten days. In this case, we can't even rely on the existence of a moment of madness or lack of control that could lead one to commit a crime. The defendant had plenty of time to repent and change his mind from what he was about to do, but instead, our murderer overloaded the dose to make sure he wouldn't fail. You ought to stop and reflect, respectable members of the jury, of the damage a person with these criminal instincts and in possession of the knowledge of such toxic substances, can cause to humanity. Given half a chance, this kind of killer can poison an entire nation and threaten the existence of all of humanity if he's got the means to do it. This is how dangerous Alfred Hayen is! Finally, I want to clarify that as far as I'm concerned, fame, economic and social status are worthless. I place honor above anything else. I have never accused anyone without being totally sure they are guilty of the offense for which they were tried. Moreover I strongly believe that an honest man's life is invaluable for humanity and must be preserved above all else. So that you have not a shadow of a doubt about my reasoning in this trial, I must remind everyone that, at the start of my career as a prosecutor, I swore on my honor and my family, that I'd pay with my own life, any innocent blood that would be spilled due to my wrongdoings. For this reason and based on evidence presented throughout this court trial, I recommend that the full weight of the law fall on the defendant Mr. Alfred Hayen for his offences and the maximum penalty be applied: The penalty of death!"

CHAPTER XXI

The prosecutor's speech left the jury eager to hear the defense attorney's conclusions. The jury listened attentively to his words, which came loaded with a philosophical air.

"Those of you, who will condemn a person without being absolutely certain of their guilt, will be committing an act against morality and humanity. How many mistakes have been made throughout the years, for not spending more time researching cases? How many innocent people have been unjustly sentenced for crimes they did not commit, simply because the jury who found them guilty didn't have the courage to accept their incompetence when issuing the verdict? Why continue to harbor uncertainty that may cause an innocent's death or imprisonment? Why commit an act of cruelty without even intending or being aware of it? Sometimes we don't know how to overcome our fears and hide opinions that perhaps, if we express them could help restart the analysis of a case which could prove the innocence of a defendant, attenuate the sentence, or bring us absolute certainty of their guilt. An honest and decent person should never allow doubt to rest on his shoulders. This case began with two defendants. Mrs. Mary Gautal, whose nerves collapsed due to the unbearably tense moments she went through in this court. If she had retained her emotional balance, she would not have made such a drastic decision. Her physical death is irreparable; but not her moral death. Clearing her name depends on you. If Mr. Alfred Hayen were to be found guilty of murder, Mrs. Mary Gautal will also appear guilty. There's still time to rescue a human being from a fate that so far only appearances condemn! You can still save both defendants from dishonor and shame! May God enlighten your judgment and allow you to reach a just verdict!"

CHAPTER XXII

The jurors were sitting around the rectangular table in the middle of the room. Refreshments were served to each. The foreman of the jury, Dr. George Levin, knew that the others waited for him to start, but before sitting down he decided to say a few words.

"Members of the jury; the pinnacle of this process has come. I would remind you what is expected of us, but the judge already did recently; but I wish that each of you keep this in mind during the deliberations. As everyone has seen, they provided us with refreshments, something unusual in judicial processes, but I imagine it has been done in order to isolate us from any possible influence that we might receive with reference to this case, if we leave these premises. At first I thought that we should express our views over lunch; but now I suggest we take twenty minutes for lunch and during that time, study and meditate individually on the case. At the end of that time, I'll ask for your opinion. If we all agree on the same verdict, we will communicate it immediately; but if there are differences of opinion, we shall remain here and deliberate until a verdict is reached. If everyone agrees with my plan, I propose to start the lunch break."

***

The silence was complete. The foreman of the jury, a dentist by profession, Dr. George Levin, kept thinking from the beginning of the case about the future of his young daughters. Since they were very small, he had always toiled in his mind with the idea that one day someone would plan to take advantage of them, but he knew that he could do nothing to prevent it. The case he was now involved in was sharpening his worries. Sometimes he even went as far as thinking that the whole thing was a premonition meant to be a wakeup call for him to stop enjoying the present and go back to worrying about the future. As for Mr. Alfred Hayen's culpability, for him it was crystal clear; not a shadow of a doubt; all evidence pointed against him. His verdict would be: "Guilty!"

***

Being part of a jury responsible for a murderer's fate by arsenic poisoning, accounted for almost an adventure for. Dr. Robert Lamart, a retired doctor who has been an example of selflessness, professionalism and dedication throughout his career. He devoted his whole life to alleviating the suffering of his fellow beings. Therefore, he couldn't understand the feelings that had driven those people to commit such a terrible crime. In his opinion, the murderers had no reservations when submitting and subjecting others to suffering immense dangers in order to cover their crime. He recapped in silence again and again, the reports submitted to the court in connection with the case. Undoubtedly, the help of medical science had proved decisive in the process, he thought, while a sense of immense pride ran through him. He took a small bite of his sandwich and said to himself sententiously: "Guilty!"

***

Miss Heddy Hill, a single woman and co-owner of a florist shop, the situation was more than clear. She was sure that the defendant had created chaos in the lives of his wife and his stepdaughter, meddling with the fate of their family. Regardless of the fact that she hated men who abused women, for her, the evidence presented against the defendant was strong and irrefutable. Mrs. Mary Gautal's suicide made it clear. She didn't expect any of the jurors to defend Mr. Alfred Hayen, but if someone wanted to side with him, she was ready to argue that in fact there were three, not two victims of that villain. She gently dried her lips with a napkin, pushed her lunch service away and leaned against the back of the chair waiting for the moment when she would be asked for the verdict: "Guilty!"

***

Mr. Norman Birman, as a nurse, he has always felt a deep respect for the human life. His twenty year career has convinced him that the most precious gift of a human being is its life. That is perhaps the reason for being elected as a member of the jury. He bit into the sandwich mechanically. His gaze fixed on the little flowers that adorned the edge of the plate which betrayed his distant mind. Recalling the case facts was hogging his attention. Once finished the last bite of his sandwich, he took out a cigarette from the case he carried inside his jacket pocket, put the cigarette to his lips, lit it, took a long puff and slowly let out the smoke. There was no doubt, he thought. The evidence, the witnesses and especially the Manual of Pharmacology, were screaming guilty. Although he understood that Mr. Alfred Hayen was a dangerous criminal, he could not but admire him for the intelligence, the courage and skill to devise prepare and execute such a crime aiming to leave no traces. He's a genius, he said to himself, but an evil genius. My verdict must be: "Guilty!"

***

Mr. Richard Baxter still didn't understand the reason why he had to leave his confinement. He could not understand why he had to get out and show his burned face and his mutilated hand in public. The explosion registered during the detonation of a bomb had marked him for life, "bloody soldiers," he said. Everything was over for him. The prosecution had provided too much evidence and data to delay for twenty minutes reaching a verdict. Moreover, he was not willing to allow anyone to see the horrible grimaces that his face would assume when putting on his mask. He glanced at the clock hanging on the wall, as if trying to rush the movement of its hands, while in his mind he only repeated one word: "Guilty! Guilty!"

***

Mr. Peter Marshel felt that the appointment to serve British justice brought him prestige among his workshop colleagues and among his relatives. Now he dressed daily in a jacket and met with people whom his mates would label as important. He thought that Mr. Alfred Hayen was a good man. A fallen victim to circumstances, but his intuition told him that no one else shared his opinion in that place and that ought not to go against them, so he decided to keep silent until he it was his turn to say: "Guilty!"

***

Mrs. Betty O'Brien, the executive secretary ate slowly, as someone who has nothing to worry about and nothing to think of. Inwardly, she thought she had done her work during the trial relying on her knowledge of psychology acquired during her Sunday morning reading. According to her insights, fear and confusion dominated Alfred Hayen's face throughout the trial and these feelings were those of someone who fears the blame for a committed crime. She also believed that since the defendant himself admitted that he expects to be convicted because his guilt was evident due to irrefutable laboratory tests, statements of witnesses, possession of the Treaty of Pharmacology and his love affair with the landlady, he must be right. She finished lunch and decided to assume an upright position in her chair, as she did in the office until she would be asked for the verdict, at which she would simply say: "Guilty!"

***

Mrs. Ann Francy, the teacher showed concern. Perhaps it was the lack of contact with her children and students. From the start of the trial her health was not well. Severe headaches tormented her especially when little Annie's name was being mentioned in the room. She believed that children represented the essence of life, virtue, purity, the unmistakable image of sublimity and love that should reign over the Earth. She couldn't find the reason why Annie had been killed. Every time she thought about her children or students, she couldn't conceive that anyone could undermine the life of a defenseless child. When she recalled their laughter resounding through the corridors, crossing walls, filling spaces, comforting sorrows, she was assured that only a coward would take a child's life. 'Alfred Hayen is guilty, everything indicates so', she thought. 'It has been proven during the trial' she agreed to herself. 'When they ask for my verdict I'll simply say: Guilty!'

***

Widow, pensioned, without family, childless, Mrs. Mary Bence had poured all her love towards her six cats. At first she had the impression that the defendants were innocent. Unfortunately, after hearing the testimonies and after having seen them hug, her opinion about them had changed. For her, any doubt as to the relationship between those two people was gone. She ended her brief lunch and opened her purse to extract a napkin. She unfolded it carefully, and then wrapped the piece of candy she had been served with her lunch. When she completed this task she felt all eyes were on her: "It's for my kittens, you know," she said apologetically. "They love the sweets." Everyone smiled. She closed her purse and began to wait patiently to be asked for the verdict. She would definitely say: "Guilty!"

***

Mr. John Kirby had spent more than two thirds of his life reading and researching about police issues behind the counter of his used book store. From what he learned from his readings, the criminal was a cold, callous, calculating and ruthless person, a pattern that didn't quite correspond to the defendants. In the early stages of the case, he thought that perhaps they had fallen victims to circumstances, but as the witnesses were submitting their declarations, his verdict changed until the prosecutor made sure he would clear away any shadow of doubt when he presented the Manual of Pharmacology as evidence. In his opinion, they committed the crime and when they were discovered, they tried to confuse everyone by masking their true personalities. Now his literary experience shouted at him: "Guilty!"

***

Mr. Michael Frechnell felt victim to a nervous imbalance: personal problems, health issues and business stress were worsening as the legal process progressed. His businesses were neglected, his health needed care and his family was nagging for a vacation. Mr. Frechnell did not expect such a long trial, but had acknowledged the complexity of the matter and the cruelty with which the crime has been committed. It wasn't like he had to judge people who have acted as a result of a breakdown, anger or frustration, he told himself. These are born criminals; people capable of everything to achieve an objective. At times he recalled the currents in Spanish rivers full of trout and felt melancholic. He recalled how the fish were fighting for their life, jumping vigorously out of the water in their desperate struggle to loosen the hook. The process had been long but it was almost over, he thought. Just imagine the water pressure on rubber pants, his hand wearied by manipulating the rod, the smell of grass, the countryside with its wild fruits, hearing the rush of water from the short waterfall, the gentle caress of the warm breeze. Maybe in a few hours he can be right there, he encouraged himself. He stopped daydreaming and settled into the chair, waiting patiently for the Dr. Levin's question that would give him back his freedom, the question to which he had the answer: "Guilty!"

***

Miss Joan Oliver didn't understand why a person of her status and class had been asked for assistance in such a trivial and mundane matter. In vain she had tried to find a way to be exempted from having to exercise her civic duty towards society. She was appalled by the petty lunch, the poor quality of the people around her, the ridiculousness of the case on trial. She was tired of all the nonsense about the dead girl and the relations between the defendants.

She wished to be able to leave immediately to escape the crushing reality ... A voice interrupted her contemplation:

"Miss Oliver, for the second time I am asking you for your verdict!" Dr. George Levin said.

"Excuse me, Dr. Levin. Excuse me", she said to promptly announce: "Guilty!"

CHAPTER XXIII

It was almost dawn. Sir Ralf Wilcot dressed hurriedly. He buttoned his shirt and knotted his tie. He adjusted his vest, buttoned it and put on his jacket. He took one last look in the mirror. Once satisfied with his appearance, he picked up the raincoat and the hat from the hanger, grabbed the umbrella and took to the street in search of his car. The morning was cold and damp. A dense fog reduced the driver's visibility to less than two meters. A leaden gray colored roof served as the sky. The fog made him drive slower than usual and he worried that he was going to be late. Sir Ralf Wilcot stopped his car in front of a solid iron gate that prevented him from continuing ahead. Sir Ralf Wilcot was greeted by the policeman on guard while opening the gate. He parked his car in the courtyard and with an agile step went to the prison's offices. He exchanged greetings with several agents and went on to meet up with the prison director, who was waiting impatiently. Sir Ralf Wilcot sat before him.

Mr. Alfred Hayen was sitting in his bed in his cell, wrapped in conversation with the prison's chaplain. Outside, a guard was waiting for orders. Sir Ralf Wilcot's arrival, accompanied by the director and two other men, interrupted the dialogue. They unlocked the gate and after a few minutes, the entourage accompanied Mr. Alfred Hayen through the wide corridor leading to the prison's courtyard. Sir Ralf Wilcot slowed down along with the rest of the group, while the Chaplin and Mr. Alfred Hayen exchanged their final words. With a nod, the chaplain gave permission for the condemned to be led to the platform. Once there, the executioner placed Alfred's head in the gallows adjusted the noose around his neck and walked slowly toward the lever which would release the trap door. Meanwhile, Alfred Hayen's voice was heard to say:

"Look at your doings Prosecutor! Contemplate your masterpiece and don't be ashamed! It's your victory! The triumph of your vanity over an innocent's life! Look at me, prosecutor! Look…"

Then, there was silence. The executioner had released the trap and the body of the condemned was hanging from the rope. The sentence had been carried out.

On his way back to his office, Sir Ralf Wilcot was meditating on Alfred's last words. Alfred Hayen had never admitted his guilt, although every piece of evidence pointed towards him. He wondered again why Mr. Alfred Hayen had wasted his last wish on asking for the prosecutor to be present at the execution. He waved it off. The murder at 113 Lombard Street was now a closed case.

CHAPTER XXIV

Inspector Joe Fort sat in the car as Harold drove at high speed through the streets of London. It was four o'clock in the afternoon four days after Alfred Hayen's execution. Harold stopped the car in front of Sir Ralf Wilcot's residence and Inspector Fort abandoned the car. He literally had to shove and push his way through the onlookers. Photographers and reporters crowded outside the entrance of the mansion. Once he could reach the path lined with flowers leading to the front door, he quickened his step further so he could cover the distance as quickly as possible to the main entrance. The prosecutor's home office was illuminated. Without hesitation, the inspector crossed the threshold of the door, knowing the pathetic scenario that waited inside. On the floor, Sir Ralf Wilcot's body lay face down. A small-caliber pistol was imprisoned between clenched fingers of the man who, during his life, has been considered one of the great values of British jurisprudence. Inspector Fort approached the body to carefully observe the hole that the bullet left in the prosecutor's right temple. A trickle of blood, still wet indicated that the act had occurred recently. Once recovered from the impression, he faced the man who stood beside the body and asked.

"Are you the family doctor?"

"Yes, Inspector," the man answered laconically.

"How long has it been since the event occurred?"

"About one hour."

"Was he already dead when you first arrived?"

"His death was instantaneous. When I arrived, there was nothing to be done. I decided to stay to wait for you due to the dismal state of Miss Elizabeth Wilcot," said the doctor, pointing to the place where the prosecutor's sister was sitting.

Inspector Fort went towards her. She greeted him politely. He took one of the woman's hands in his, by way of consolation and adherence to her grief and, looking into her eyes, said in a compassionate tone:

"There's nothing we can do now, Miss. Wilcot. We have to take life as it comes."

The lady embraced the inspector. She leaned her head on his shoulder and began to cry. A shudder shook her body. Inspector Fort gently pushed her away.

"Crying won't bring him back Miss Wilcot. Your brother has been a good friend to me but we must overcome our loss because now it's very important to try and find out the reasons that led him to make such a drastic decision. This is the reason why I'll kindly ask you to retire to your room, while I take care of everything."

On the prosecutor's desk, there was an envelope addressed to inspector Joe Fort. Inspector Fort, picked it up, opened it, took out the letter inside and began to read:

Dear Friend:

Don't judge my actions without previously having read this letter. Analyze it and, being the honorable man you are, I believe you will understand me.

Today around eleven thirty, I received a phone call from my good friend Mr. Lewis Thompson, editor of The London Observer. He asked me to go to his office immediately at the journal's headquarters, given the importance of the matter he had to discuss with me. I agreed to go immediately and meet him and so I did.

When I arrived at his office, I found him in the company of an elderly lady. Mr. Thompson asked me to take a seat in front of him. He then handed me an envelope, which was already opened having previously been sealed with wax and proceeded to explain that the lady had made a trip all the way from France only to bring me the letter. According to her, the letter had reached her hands inside another envelope containing express instructions from her niece Mrs. Luisa Lonfard, a few days after her death in hospital.

She, serving the posthumous wishes of her deceased niece, was instructed to save the letter until Mr. Alfred Hayen fulfilled the sentence that may have been imposed on him in connection with her death and that of little Annie. In the event that the sentence was too long or that she fell ill, she should appoint another person to fulfill the task. However, should Mr. Alfred Hayen be acquitted or should he manage to avoid a trial for murder, Luisa's instructions had been to burn the letter in the fire without anyone reading it.

According to Mr. Thompson, Mrs. Annie Lonfard was waiting to deliver the letter personally, until late morning. She refused, at all times, to leave the letter with any other person who would promise to deliver it for her and was very specific in pointing out that the newspaper that was to publish the letter had been selected by her niece due to their trustworthiness and wide reach. Mr. Thompson then asked the lady to identify herself fully and as soon as his request has been satisfied, he proceeded to read the letter. When Mr. Thompson finished reading, he understood its impact it would have on me which is why he called me to invite me to his office urgently.

While reading the letter, I could not believe what was written there. I finished reading and asked Mr. Thompson to withhold publication until a later date as I had to solve some issues of vital importance and the publication of the letter before that would surely prevent me doing so. Mr. Thompson, as a good friend, accepted because he had the right to first publication assured.

I also requested to submit the letter to the expertise of a calligrapher, in order to dispel any possible doubt regarding the authenticity, since I already had in my possession some notes written by Mrs. Luisa Hayen, which I had collected on my visit to 113 Lombard Street, and could compare those to the letter in order to establish its legitimacy. Once the three of us agreed, we called the expert calligrapher Mr. Olaf Slovant, from the technical department of Scotland Yard, who invited us to go to his offices with the material to be investigated. Then I signed a document which recognized the existence of the letter, its content and my commitment to return it to the newspaper, on the same afternoon, all at Mrs. Annie Lonfard's insistence and for her peace of mind.

With the letter allegedly written by Mrs. Luisa Hayen and

the brief notes I had from the guest house, which I had absolute certainty that had been written by herself, I went to see Mr. Slovant. A short time after, he determined that whoever had written the notes was also the author of the letter.

I name my sister Elizabeth as my universal heir and I truly hope she will find it in her heart to forgive my action.

Finally, I would like to ask you for one last favor. After you have read Mrs. Luisa Hayen's letter which you'll find in the top drawer of the right tower of my desk, I beg you to send it immediately to Mr. Lewis Thompson, the editor of The London Observer. Thank you.

Your friend,
Sir Ralf Wilcot

CHAPTER XXV

Inspector Joe Fort placed the letter his late friend wrote on the desk. He rubbed his eyes trying to relieve them from tiredness and put his hand on the handle of the drawer indicated in the letter. He opened it and took out the envelope Sir Ralf Wilcot referred to in his farewell note.

To whom it may concern:

I met Alfred some time ago, through a friend of my late husband. He was recommended to me as the person who could help me administer the property that I inherited when I was widowed. Some time later, Alfred and I got married.

The financial state of my estate worsened under Alfred's management and to avoid his imprisonment, I agreed to sell the house we lived in, which was part of my inheritance and we took accommodation in a guest house owned by Mrs. Mary Gautal.

After a few months of living in the guesthouse, I realized that my husband was having an affair with Mrs. Gautal. I didn't say anything, but I began to watch their every move until I had no doubt that they were indeed lovers. A deep desire for revenge, edging towards madness, took hold of me.

I dismissed the idea of killing them with my own hands, because I thought that the suffering I would cause them this way would not be enough. In addition, my little Annie would have to live her entire life with the stigma of being the daughter of a murderer. There were many ways to take revenge on them, but I chose one that would cause them the most suffering and frustration leaving them helpless and incapable of escape.

I was deep in thoughts and depression when I stumbled upon a treaty of pharmacology, which Alfred assiduously read, in search for a sexual stimulant. Among those pages, I found what seemed to be the escape from my problems. A plan quickly crystallized in my mind so I immediately prepared a trip to France, supposedly to visit Aunt Annie. On this trip, I would have the best opportunities to obtain everything I needed to carry out the plan, without arousing any suspicions.

Once in France, I visited the practice of a doctor in a small village, far away from where Aunt Annie lived. Fortunately the doctor turned out to be an older man who had, after practicing his profession in Paris for over forty years, decided to seek peace and tranquility in the province.

To his questions regarding the reasons for my visit, I answered that I decided to consult him at the recommendation of a friend who had talked to me about her success in the treatment of asthenia, using arsenic.

Since there aren't any people in the world who can escape the sin of vanity prompted by praise, the doctor proceeded to give me a detailed explanation on the matter and he even insisted to show me the literature on the subject for which he went looking in an adjoining room; I took the opportunity of these moments of solitude to pinch a bunch of prescriptions with his letterhead from his desk.

I left his practice with what I needed. Then I copied the formula provided by the doctor on several prescriptions. To avoid suspicion I went from town to town, asking various pharmacies to prepare the prescriptions until I was in possession of the necessary amount of the formula to carry out my plans.

I passed through customs with the medicine hidden in a double bottom made in my handbag, so the officer in charge of checking the luggage, didn't notice it.

Back in 113 Lombard Street, I started implementing my plan. I provided the first dose of the drug and started complaining of the rat problem so that Mrs. Gautal, knowing that Alfred had knowledge of how to prepare an arsenic based paste that would be effective as a rat poison, would ask him to do just that.

Alfred brought arsenic and prepared rat poison with half of the purchased product, giving Mrs. Gautal the other half, to safeguard it. I took out the rest and replaced it with common talc, which I spilled into the rubbish bin.

The next day I increased the dose as it was indicated the prescription, which read: "Start with one drop a day and keep adding a daily drop until you reach twenty. After reaching this amount, decrease the dose in the same way, reducing a daily drop of medicine. This methodology should be followed rigorously, because if misused can cause severe poisoning that can lead to death."

During the first twelve days of arsenic working in the bodies of Paul and Jeannie Donalt as well as in Mrs. Gautal and in Alfred no major setbacks were noticed. Only the Donalts were a bit indisposed but fortunately everything passed.

As for myself, I must admit that I have faced times when I lacked the strength to carry on; I even considered abandoning my plan altogether and try to work things out with Alfred. But, last night when I pleaded with him to leave the guest house with me and go in search of happiness elsewhere, he bluntly refused. I decided to stick to my plan and now I am simply waiting for the celebration dinner tonight to end this nightmare. It's too late now to repent and turn back. All I want is to make them suffer with my sacrifice.

If my plan were to fail, this letter shall never be read by anyone, for I have given instructions to be burned. But if all goes as I planned, you dear first reader, will witness what damage a hurt woman's desire for vengeance can cause. And so will the readers of your newspaper.

Tonight, some time after dinner, all the inhabitants of the house will suffer due to arsenic poisoning. As a result of it, my little Annie and I will die. The rest will be ill for a while but they will survive due to the tolerance that I have created in their bodies, during the previous weeks.

The police investigation will aim to understand how the poisoning occurred and what the poisonous substance was, and then they'll search for murder motives. Alfred doesn't lack reasons to get rid of me and I also took care that both of them bought arsenic, which can engage them further.

I hope that, if everything goes as I've planned, both of them will be tried for murder. In recent days I have been informing the neighbors about the intimate relationship between Alfred and Mrs. Gautal and about the ruin that Alfred's management had caused to my finances.

This will be my revenge: they will be judged and convicted for a crime that they did not commit and they will be incapable of defending themselves. I hope they will be sentenced to many years in prison and later upon their release they'll come across this letter. What greater punishment can be there for what they've done to me?

For my part, I see no reason whatsoever to continue to exist, being penniless and having nowhere to go. As for Annie, what would she do without me? Who would take care of her? Who would love her as I do?

I believe that this is all I have to say. I trust that Aunt Annie will comply with my instructions. I will close the envelope containing this letter with sealing wax and post it, along with the instructions inside another envelope. I'll also take the opportunity to get rid of the last empty bottle of arsenic and the rat poison paste that Alfred prepared, which I replaced with a paste made from talc powder in order to facilitate the work of the police.

For the same reason, tonight I plan to burn, in Mrs. Gautal's compact powder box the rest of that first purchase of arsenic which got lost, because it's possible to identify the product from waste paper or tissue even when they're burned together. To avoid the smell of burnt paper I'll gift Alfred a box of Turkish cigarettes after dinner, as their scent will dominate the air.

I'll put the treaty of pharmacology, carefully read by Alfred, in a place where it would stand out in case Alfred chooses not to read it tonight. If he'll choose to stick with his reading custom tonight, he'll surely leave it in the appropriate place for the police to find it and this will further help my plans.

Now, all that's left for me to do is to wait for dinner. My biggest regret is the short life that my little Annie has enjoyed.

Mrs. Luisa Hayen.